Cupid

AND

Cupcakes

KIRI PATTERSON

Published Independently

ISBN: 979-8-9906373-2-0

Cover design by Kiri Patterson

Edited by Emily Cutler

For permissions, inquiries, or more information, contact: authorkiripatterson@gmail.com

To my mother, Betty Adamson—
Finding you the happily ever after you deserve will always be one of my goals.
Thank you for inspiring my love of reading, for always believing I could achieve the world, and, most of all, for showing me what it means to be a loving mother.

To mothers—motherhood is the most challenging and most rewarding thing I've ever experienced. I hope you give yourself grace as you find your way along its bumpy path.

Chapter One

THE PINK CARDBOARD BOX ON MY COUNTER PROMISED sweet distraction. Bribery, courtesy of Jane—three cupcakes for thirty minutes on a dating app.

I grabbed the red velvet cupcake and sat, twisting on my pink leather swivel stool, peeling down the cupcake wrapper and licking red frosting from my fingertips. Sugar melted on my tongue, whispering that this was totally worth the sacrifice.

I picked up my phone and mentally prepared myself for the upcoming photoshopped abs and creepy innuendo taglines.

Bachelor #1— Caught an enormous fish...nice.

Swipe.

Bachelor #2— Oh! What a cute dog. I clicked through a few pictures, desperately searching for more of the fuzzy white-and-brown puppy. After a few more pics, including one with him in a full Darth Vader costume, it was easy to see I was far more interested in spending time with the dog than him.

Swipe.

Why wouldn't Jane and Mom accept that I was done dating?

Matchmaking for someone else, though...that was the best. The only problem was the dismal number of single friends I had.

Bachelor #3— Rocking some dangerously short gym shorts and a tank top lifted to show some very nice abs. "Looking for a hottie with a rockin' gym body."

I finished my cupcake. Call me crazy, but I don't think we would "work out"—pun intended. I was more comfort curves than chiseled lines.

Swipe.

It would be another five minutes before Leo's Pasta got here. I brushed the cupcake crumbs from the counter and my silk Elvis pajama pants, right onto the floor for Future Me to worry about. I hopped off the stool and walked the six whole steps to the middle of the living room to my green mid-century modern couch. My apartment in downtown Boise, Idaho, lacked extra square footage, but I made up for it with my fifties flair. I plopped down on the couch and my phone vibrated with an incoming text.

Jane: Any winners yet???

If I'd have known she would be so insistent on double-dating, I would have left her single. I cringed. Not that the setup had been all for Jane's benefit... When Finn's mother had come into the store asking about setting me up with her son, I knew she needed to be pointed in a different direction—Jane's direction.

Emma: Um... Maybe?

Jane: Did you even look at it for more than 5 minutes?

Emma: You know I was so distracted. I actually spent 35. =P

Jane: Liar.

I shrugged. Worth a shot.

Jane: I mean it! Emma, those cupcakes were for bribery only!! If you don't spend 30 minutes looking for a date, then you will pay me back. I expect you to interact with at least five guys...

Jane: Don't make me come over there.

Jane lived in an apartment about fifteen minutes away, so it wasn't an idle threat. She'd face the spring rain without a second thought.

I leaned my head back onto the cushion and closed my eyes.

I could admit it. "The problem" might very well be me.

I was a bit eccentric. I glanced over at my teal blue fridge and pink-suitcase vinyl player. The "normal life" just didn't appeal to me. I'd chosen to forgo college despite scholarships, my obsession with the fifties and old movies was borderline crazy, and I'm pretty sure my type of man went extinct along with rotary phones. I wanted a black and white movie type of romance with old-fashioned manners, big romantic gestures, and a serenade or two.

It was a bit unusual for a twenty-two-year-old woman, but it wasn't entirely my fault. Like most new adults with issues, I blamed my mother.

In the fifth grade, Brad and I had been soul mates. I even had a notebook where I practiced my signature with my future last name. Then, I caught him sharing his Gatorade and his lips with my best friend Savannah.

He was my first heartbreak.

That night, Mom sat next to me on the couch while we ate ice cream and watched black and white movies full of men performing grand romantic gestures. That night a tradition was born: Cary Grant movie dates, either alone or with mom, after each lousy boyfriend. And there were plenty of lousy boyfriends.

Maybe I was a novelty—fun at first, but the charm wore off fast.

I reached over the arm of the couch to the basket of blankets and pulled off the top one.

My relationships all started great, but then it would start to shift with remarks about my style, movie choice, my love of sweets, and my "unique" personality. I found myself tempted to shift. To change so they might want to stay. After my last boyfriend, I decided I was done. It was too hard to try to choose between loving me or being with a man... I chose me.

My phone vibrated.

Jane: I'm coming over if you haven't texted in five minutes with a name and profile pic you are considering.

I refocused on the app and scrolled mindlessly through the singles within a twenty-mile radius, willing the clock to move faster.

I had no desire to date. Playing Cupid was my new life mission, but I would scroll a few minutes for cupcakes.

An ad popped up and covered Bachelor #4 and his cat, Sprinkles. It was advertising local events for singles that were fifty and older. Well, if that was where my man was, that would be discouraging.

I checked the clock and decided time counted as double when on a dating app. I took a screenshot and zoomed in around the cat Sprinkles.

Emma: So far, this one is the most promising. =)

A knock sounded at the door.

Leo's was early!

I grabbed my purse hanging next to my jacket and keys underneath the black and white movie poster of *My Favorite Wife*. I looked up at Cary Grant kissing Irene Dunn. If people could wish on a star, then a Cary Grant picture should count as the same thing, right?

Cary Grant light, Cary Grant bright, I wish I may, I wish I might have my own Cary Grant tonight. I chuckled at my wit.

There was an aggressive knock at the door.

Maybe they were fast because I was becoming a regular. I flinched. Was that good or bad?

Good because it was fast...but bad that an Italian restaurant knew me well enough to ask if I wanted my usual and the delivery guy knew my name. Meh.

My mouth watered at the thought of their breadsticks. I fished my wallet from my purse and swung the door open.

I stepped back.

Not Leo's.

Mom stood on the doorstep with her graying shoulder-length hair, dark cardigan, and tan slacks. She eyed my stained pj's and greasy hair pulled into a ponytail, her lips pulled down into a frown.

"Mom?" I was sure she had plans tonight with Betty and the other Bunco ladies. "Why are you here?"

She stepped into the apartment. "Now, is that any way to greet your mother?" She leaned in for a hug and a not too subtle sniff.

"Mom... I shower regularly. It's Saturday. Pj's are an all-day requirement." I stepped back, giving mom room to step into my apartment.

"I was thinking we could go out tonight." Mom could not stand my current weekend routine or lack thereof. I could admit it, I'd been in a funk, but it was because I hadn't found my next Cupid project. Romance paints the world in bright colors, and finding that light for others made me happy.

I walked toward the kitchen. "I thought you had plans tonight?"

"I thought we could have plans. Betty's son is working at the new pizza place in Indian Creek Plaza. How about we go there?"

"Really?" My face pulled down in a frown. "Brett? Didn't he just graduate?" I grimaced, thinking about his ungodly height and love of Pokémon.

"Oh, he's not that bad. He's better than the guys you have been dating." She placed her hands on her hips.

"Mom, I graduated four years ago. I'm not interested in Brett, and I'm not sure he's even legal." I set my wallet down on the counter and opened the pink box, showing her the last two cupcakes inside. This was the fastest way to end this conversation. My sugar addiction came straight from my mama.

"Well, I don't see you with any other options." She looked tired. I wondered if they had her working double shifts again at the packaging factory. I didn't remember my dad enough to miss him, but I wished he had stuck around, if only so mom didn't have to work so hard.

"And since I have sworn off dating entirely, that will continue." I walked back to Mom and held out the cupcake bribe.

Mom sighed, but grabbed the pink cupcake with sprinkles. "It's time to put yourself out there again."

I rolled my eyes. "You're one to talk."

My mother had been single for twenty years, and I didn't see her lining up to get in the dating ring.

She huffed and took a small bite out of her cupcake. "We have been over this. It's different. My life is plenty full and busy with you kiddos."

The problem was, her little kiddos had grown up. Caleb was married, living in Utah and building his MLM empire. Ivy was married with a baby and another one on the way. And I adored my independence. Mom was left working jobs to pay off past debt, sleeping in a bigger house than she needed, and hoping one of her kids would show an inclination of needing her help.

Her whole life was taking care of us, but what would she do if she was free to do anything?

"There are good guys out there." She took a bite of the cupcake and smiled. "But no good comes from staying home in your pj's all the time." She gestured to my Elvis pants.

"Something very good is coming from staying in my pj's. It's a man, an *Italian* man," I raised my eyebrows appreciatively, "and he is bringing breadsticks." I whispered.

Mom rolled her eyes and swatted my arm as I chuckled.

I bumped into her with my shoulder. "I appreciate it, but it's different, dating now. The guys are different." We walked over to the pink stools. "I'm different."

Mom sat and took a small bite of her cupcake.

"Old-fashioned manners are as extinct as dinosaurs."

She swiveled to face me. "Emma Ann Woods, you better not be comparing me to dinosaurs!"

I chuckled and rolled my eyes. "You know what I mean."

There was a knock at the door.

I tipped my head to mom. "I have *Roman Holiday* ready to play, and the best Italian food." Based on the bags under Mom's eyes, she needed a movie night more than a night out anyway. "Want to watch a movie with me?"

Her shoulders relaxed, giving up the fight. "Fine."

I smiled. Mom always was more bark than bite.

I opened the door.

"Delivery from Leo's." Peter was an older man that had kind eyes, gray hair, and a wide smile. He had brought my orders the last few months, and it was always wonderful to see him. He held up a large sack filled with pasta, breadsticks, and—as usual—dessert.

"Hey, Peter, come on in." I held the door open as he nodded and stepped into the apartment, and I grabbed some cash for a tip from my wallet. "You got another date with Cary Grant tonight?" He nodded to the TV.

"Cary Grant dates are the best!" Technically, it was Gregory Peck and Audrey Hepburn, but close enough. I counted out the cash and handed it to him.

Noticing Mom, he tipped his head, "Evening, ma'am."

She nodded. "Good evening."

Peter turned to leave. "Have a good night, Emma, and enjoy your Cary Grant." He winked.

"Oh, I will. Thanks for the food. Drive safe." I held the door for him.

I watched as he hopped down the steps. For an older man, he still had plenty of pep in his step. It was too bad Peter was married and a little too old—otherwise I would have tried to set him up with Mom. He was sweet and full of old-fashioned charm.

I watched him leave.

Wait.

That's it! I closed the door and turned back toward the kitchen, looking at the white plastic bag of food like it held answers to the universe.

That was who I should set up next—Mom!

It would be perfect.

I had loved setting up friends and coworkers, but Mom... Mom would be amazing. It was like I had been training my whole life to pull off this magical event.

What would it be like to have her be spoiled? To have someone sweep her off her feet and make her life easier? I envisioned some silver-haired man in a Corvette driving her through France. I resisted the urge to clap and squeal, but the shoulder shimmy couldn't be contained.

She raised her eyebrow. "Are you that excited for Leo's?"

We moved to the kitchen and I set the bag on the counter. I opened the cupboard next to the sink, grabbed out two glass plates, and started loading them up with the steaming cheese ravioli and breadsticks. "Are you not?" I scoffed.

She rolled her eyes and grabbed a few dishes from the sink and started rinsing them off to put in the dishwasher. She couldn't help it. If she was awake, she felt like she should be helping.

But who was helping her?

"Mom, remember, no cleaning."

"Oh, it was just a few dishes." Mom shrugged me off.

"A few dishes that *I* will clean. Later." I eyed her until she stopped.

"Oh fine. It's not a big deal." She huffed.

I wouldn't mind the help from time to time. The problem was, from sunup to sundown, she couldn't stop working. I wanted her to relax. "Let's watch the movie."

I nodded to her plate. She picked it up and followed me to the couch. I pushed play on *Roman Holiday* and the instrumental intro came to life.

"I love this one." Mom was smiling and leaning toward me as the opening credits played.

"Same." Audrey Hepburn played a princess on the run who fell for an undercover journalist.

I could picture it now, except with Mom in place of Audrey.

Mom, driving through Rome, being swept off her feet in a big romantic gesture. I drummed my fingers on my leg.

What had that ad said? Something about fifty plus... Mom had just turned fifty-one.

She wouldn't like it at first, but I doubted she would complain in the long run.

I grabbed my phone and found the ad. It took me to a website called "Kismet Silvers." I peeked over at Mom to see her already sinking deeper into the cushions. I wondered if she'd make it twenty minutes before she fell asleep.

My screen filled with a picture of an older couple lying on a sunny beach in lounge chairs, toasting fruity drinks.

Yep. This was perfect!

I had bugged her about dating before, but she always said she didn't have time, or didn't want the drama. I was giddy at the thought of my mom in love.

I scrolled the page. Events were held at The Brick House, newly remodeled. You signed up for an account and could purchase tickets to local events for other "Silver Singles." I adjusted so my phone was faced away from Mom. This would be way easier than trying to set her up on dates secretly. This could work.

I clicked on the calendar.

The events included food, meet and greets, book clubs, dances, and vintage movie days.

She would never do this on her own. I chewed my lip.

I glanced sideways at Mom, who was seconds from sleep. My finger hovered over the bright red "Join Now" button at the bottom of the mobile page. I clicked it.

A screen popped up.

"Please be aware this is for fifty plus only. By clicking accept, you acknowledge you are aware of these rules and you are over fifty."

If anyone deserved a happily ever after, it was Mom, and I would do anything to get it for her.

Accept.

Chapter Two

I turned on the lights and switched the sign to OPEN at The Bees Knees. I started working here three days after I graduated high school, and I'd loved all four years at this second-hand store with its blend of shabby chic meets vintage. The store was owned by Wanda, but she had let me put my stamp on the place and had hinted about retiring soon.

Ivy said I would be crazy to think I could invest in and run a business at my age, but then again, she also thought giving up my scholarships was a terrible idea as well.

The first thing I added to the store was a vintage media section complete with movie posters, old film reels, signed pictures, and anything else I could get my hands on.

I passed the large traveling trunks, old medicinal bottles, and blue-and-white china dishes on the refurbished vanity toward the back of the shop. I grabbed a stack of vinyl records and picked Elvis. I pulled out the black disk and put it under the needle. If there was a place that felt like home, other than my apartment, it was here. It was a hug from the past. A past that I wished to belong to.

The bell over the door facing Main Street rang. Jane rushed

toward me. She was dressed in pink leggings and running shoes with her gorgeous long hair pulled back in a slick ponytail. Jane never needed help in the dating department, but I gave it to her willingly anyway.

She jogged up to the counter. "Hey, Em, I need to borrow the bathroom."

"Too much green smoothie?" I grinned and handed her the key.

She grimaced. "Okay, it has its downsides. But I promise it tastes better than it looks."

I'd seen her prep this "magic" smoothie as she added spinach, banana, and cottage cheese to a blender. She tried to get me to taste it. She failed. There was no way it tasted edible.

I shuddered as I remembered the green slimy mixture. "I don't believe you."

She rolled her eyes. But the need for the bathroom must have been greater than for defending the green drink. She rushed past me.

I grabbed a box and restocked the jars of penny candies and flavored honey. A notification sounded on my phone, and I pulled it from the back pocket of my jeans. It was from Kismet Silvers saying new profiles were live. I'd already uploaded a photo of Mom in a 1920s flapper dress and a bright smile.

I sat in my favorite chair in the furniture section, a velvet gold swivel that hugged around my back. It would only take a few minutes to glance through Mom's new dating prospects.

Too bald.

Not enough teeth.

Too many wrinkles.

Hmm... This one says he has a horse ranch. That could be cool. Mom loved horses, but she didn't have the time or means to own one.

I hearted the profile and heard a gasp over my shoulder. I

turned to see Jane staring at my phone, her mouth opened and her eyes wide.

"What are you doing?" Jane glanced around the store to make sure we were alone and reached for my phone.

I moved my hand out of her reach.

"When I said to see which fish were in the sea, I didn't mean the Dead Sea!" She held her hand out for my phone. "Let me see it. You must have changed some setting or something, because this group has gone seriously over the hill."

She thought I was looking for myself. I handed her my phone, eager to see her reaction.

"What filters are you using?" She clicked frantically on my screen.

I bit back a giggle.

"Over fifty, wealthy, travels, and owns horses." Jane faked a gag. "Em? What are you doing?" She practically threw the phone back at me, her face straight from an old, over-dramatized horror film.

I chuckled and returned to my phone. "They aren't for me."

"What?" Jane had a blank look on her face. "I mean, I'm glad, but..."

"I've decided who I'm setting up next." I did a little excited shoulder shimmy as I met her hazel eyes. "My mom!"

Jane's eyebrows furrowed, and she stepped back and put her hands on her hips. "Em, your mom would never let you set her up." Jane and I were childhood friends, and she knew Mom's fire almost as well as I did. "How did you get her to agree?"

I continued to scroll through the balding men.

"Em?" Her tone was stern.

"Fine. She doesn't know." I refused eye contact.

Jane frowned. "Your mom is gonna kill you. I think this is worse than when we decided we wanted a pink cat and spray-painted Spike."

I flinched. Mom was livid.

Would she really be that mad? I mean, I didn't think she would be happy...but when she was in Europe, she would be thanking me.

"She might not like the process, but can you imagine?" I sighed and leaned back in my chair. "She could travel, Jane, and be taken care of for once. Her whole life has been taking care of everyone else. Maybe she could even have horses again." I tried to show her the profile on my phone.

Jane shoved my phone away and started to stretch out her legs. "Wait! You promised when you took those cupcakes you would look at the dating app—"

I raised my finger. "I did."

"For *you* to find a date." She glared at me, but it was hard to take her seriously as she raised up and down on her toes, stretching out her calves.

"I looked at it for myself first, but then this ad came up for these older singles events." I stood, no longer able to hold still. "Trust me, this will be perfect. This is so much better."

Jane stopped stretching and narrowed her eyes. "Better for who?"

My finger paused above the phone. This wasn't about me. I was thinking of Mom, but I wasn't sure Jane would agree with my logic. It sounded like we were dangerously close to heading into another talk about trust, avoidance, and boundaries.

Gross.

The bell over the front door chimed as a tall man with brown hair and a black jacket walked through.

"Welcome in," I called out. He wasn't our typical customer—he was way too young, and he was way too hot. He held up his hand in a wave and flashed me a kind smile, showing a dimple on his cheek. He was probably a foot taller than me and looked like he never skipped a day at the gym. I resisted the urge to smile. I'm a sucker for a dimple.

"Can I help you find anything?" I smiled back.

He ran his hand through his chocolate brown hair and rested it on the back of his neck, effectively showing off his biceps. "Do you have a movie section?"

I nodded. "Yep! Straight up four rows and to the right."

"Thanks." He returned to his looking around the store and I did my best to return my attention to looking at Jane.

She placed her hand on the wall beside her and used it for balance as she stretched out her right leg by pulling it behind her. "How do you plan to get her on these dates, anyway?" She switched legs.

Oh right, setting up mom. For a second, tall, dark, and handsome distracted me from my goal.

"That's why this is so perfect. Look." I walked up to her, dodging the swinging legs. "They have this social section for new events." I clicked around on the website and brought up the calendar section. "It's at the remodeled venue in Eagle."

Jane leaned over and stared down at the phone.

"See? I wouldn't need to set her up on individual dates. I just need to get her there. The rest should take care of itself."

She side-eyed me, not convinced.

"Look." I clicked on the event that was in two days and read aloud. "Come meet other singles and mingle in an exclusive event for fifty and up. There will be a live band, get-to-know-you games, dance lessons, and desserts." I clicked on the buy tickets link at the bottom. "See, it even lets you get two tickets with the account, so I could go with her." I looked at Jane, unable to hold in my excitement. "They have all these themed parties. Disco night, travel the world, bingo and board games, and media blast from the past. It's perfect. She is going to have so much fun."

Jane raised an eyebrow and scrolled my phone to the part where, in bold, it said "fifty plus."

I was hoping she hadn't noticed that part.

One problem at a time.

"Mom is over fifty, and it's not like I'm looking for a date. I'm just her plus-one."

"Looks like you owe me a box of cupcakes." Jane raised an eyebrow.

"Would you even eat them?" I scoffed.

She had been on a no-sugar diet for a year now—something about sugar increasing your likelihood of disease. I swore a life without sugar wasn't worth living.

"That is beside the point." Jane nodded toward the front of the store. "How about we forget the app. Look at that guy."

I turned to see the man sifting through the media section. He shook his brown hair out of his eyes, and I had to admit he was gorgeous. Like the men they use on the weird commercials for cologne type gorgeous.

Jane leaned into me. "You ask him out, and I will forget the cupcakes."

I felt butterflies erupt in my stomach as I stared—whoa, settle. I had to admit, he was tempting. I shook my head and firmed my resolve. I was trying to focus on choosing me, and already a dimple had me considering calling it quits.

No. I was already on a mission, and that mission was Mom. "That guy is way too young for Mom." I scrunched my brows.

"Ugh! Not for your mom!" She swatted my shoulder. "I'm talking about you."

The bell over the door chimed, and we turned to see the man leaving as quick as he came. Removing any lasting temptation with him. I wasn't sure if I should feel relieved or sad. Relieved. I should feel relieved.

Jane sighed in defeat. "What am I going to do with you?" She pushed the buttons on her watch and headed toward the front. "I need to finish my run or I'm going to be late."

I followed her through the store.

Jane held the door open, "Wanna join me?" She nodded outside.

This was a long-standing joke between us, and her way of

saying she wasn't mad at me, but this discussion was not over. I accepted the peace offering.

"I totally would, but I'm working." I smiled. "Next time maybe."

"Em," She raised a brow and challenged. "Stop avoiding." She waved. "One of these times, you're going to come running. Talk later." She turned and left.

I wasn't avoiding. I wanted Mom to be happy. She deserved this. I was basically a saint, I was putting others needs first.

I looked down at the phone and added two tickets to the cart and clicked checkout.

A window popped up.

All events with Kismet Silvers are for singles fifty and up only. By clicking accept you agree the tickets are both for participants fifty plus.

"Ugh." My lips pulled down in frustration. Did it really have to say both?

What's the worst that could happen? I mean, it wasn't like I could go to jail for it. I pursed my lips and looked up to the ceiling. They might ask me to leave...but maybe I could find someone to spoil Mom before then?

I bit my thumbnail, running through the pros and cons.

Worth the risk.

I clicked the green accept button again.

Next steps: get Mom to hang out with me on Wednesday night and figure out how to look fifty.

Easy.

Chapter Three

THE BONUS OF HAVING ECLECTIC TASTE WAS THAT MY fifties style dress would fit right in at an event tailored to a much older generation. I only needed to cover my hair and face. That's what the huge sun hat in the back seat was for.

Mom came out of her large four-bedroom farmhouse in flats, a cream cardigan, and dark slacks. Her makeup was soft and subtle and she was beautiful. She was one of those best appearance forward every time she leaves the house type girls. She pulled open the door of my yellow Volkswagen Beetle and sat, placing her purse between us like she always did.

I sighed in relief. So far, so good. I peeked at her purse without being obvious, spying Mom's phone. I'd only need a few seconds to grab it and turn on airplane mode. I couldn't have her calling for reinforcements before I was ready.

"So, what do you need help with?" She grabbed her seat belt and buckled. Getting Mom to come help in a crisis was simple, getting her to stay after she realized the ruse would be the tricky part.

I had kept it vague on purpose, and said I really needed some extra help at the apartment. "Oh I have a few things to hang, and then I wanted to go through my closet." I shifted into reverse, focusing on backing out of the long gravel driveway. Her tulips were blooming, and if I ran over them, it would not put her in a good mood.

"I could have met you at the apartment." Mom shifted in her seat. She hated "being a burden," as she liked to put it.

"I know you could have, but I was already out and about." I smiled at her, not lying yet. "And you are helping me, so I'm happy to pick you up."

"You are such a sweet thing." Her eyebrow creased. "Which is why I worry about you alone in that apartment."

I rolled my eyes. "How is that any different from you being alone in a big farmhouse all the way out in Caldwell?"

She waved me off. "I'm older, it's different."

"Nope, not different. If anything, it's worse."

She might not still be thinking I was sweet here in twenty minutes. The Brick House was near Eagle, so at least it was in the same direction as my apartment. I drove into town and merged onto the freeway.

I switched lanes and topics. "So how's work?"

"It's fine. They have mandatory overtime right now."

"How are your knees?"

"My hands have been swelling a bit and my knee keeps acting up some. I guess I can't blame the floors on me being over fifty." She exhaled softly. "All in all, it's a great job with a great schedule. So I can't complain."

"Mom...can't we find you a less physically demanding job?" I hated thinking of her on her feet all day, moving heavy packages around.

"Oh, I'm fine. I don't want you worrying about me. I'm your mother and you're my daughter, not the other way around."

The guilt I'd felt before now sat comfortably behind my righteous cause. "I was hoping to stop at a building in Eagle and check if they have anything for the shop. Do you mind?"

Mom waved off my concern. "Oh, whatever you need, dear. I can't believe Ivy's baby is due next month. I'm so excited to go out and help her for a few weeks." She turned toward me as I took the Eagle exit. "Have you talked to Ivy at all lately?"

Nope.

I hadn't talked to her in a while. The last time we chatted she said if I spent more time dating and less "rummaging through old dirty objects," I could be married too. She didn't see the beauty in my store and I did not see the beauty of being married for the sake of a status symbol. If Mom knew we were fighting again, she would turn her attention to "fixing." Space would work its magic, and Ivy and I would try again later.

Some things never change, whether we were eight or twenty-eight. We were raised in the same house by Mom, but somehow we were very different people.

"I haven't called for a bit. I'll try this weekend." I lied. I needed another week at least. "I talked to Caleb last week though." By talk I meant I'd texted him and asked if he was coming home for Mom's birthday in a few months. For siblings, I thought we were decently close. We could eat Thanksgiving dinner without anyone throwing food. Seemed like a win to me.

Mom was always hoping we could be more like friends than siblings.

She nodded, satisfied that her babies were still communicating.

"How's Spike?" I was amazed the cat was still alive.

Mom sighed. "She's good, though still a terrible mouser. The other day she proudly showed me one that she brought in from outside... It was still alive. She let it go and didn't even bother to chase it as it ran around the kitchen."

"Oh no." I chuckled as she told me about Spike's new adventures and the Bunco group's newest addition. I pulled into The Brick House's parking lot. I had been seeing stuff about the renovations for a bit and was excited to go inside. All three floors' interior lights were shining through the oversized windows set in a dark red brick exterior.

Mom turned and looked at the building. "Did you know this used to be a potato processing plant?"

I used her momentary distraction into the past to grab her phone and turn on airplane mode. Electronics were not her strong suit and it would take her a while to figure out what was wrong. I slipped the phone back in her purse.

"Nancy mentioned they had to shut down again for several months. Something about water problems." She tapped her fingers on her leg. "Her son had his reception scheduled here, but they had to cancel at the last minute. She was livid." Mom turned and faced me. "Informed us we were now boycotting the place."

"Yep." I grabbed my gray eyeliner from my purse and added light lines around my eyes and near my mouth. I tried to look at my face from different directions. It wasn't great.

Mom scowled in my direction. "Em?" She leaned in. "Are you drawing wrinkle lines on your face?"

I jerked mid wrinkle line, causing a dark smudge. "No, um, it's a new contour shading thing I saw online. Do you like it?" I gave up with the pencil and grabbed the large floppy sun hat from the back seat and began securing my light blond hair underneath it with pins. Mom leaned out of the way of the large brim.

"Honestly, no." Mom held her hands up to protect her face. "It looks terrible." She started digging in her purse. "Don't worry, I should have a wet wipe in here."

I hopped out of the car before she could attack. "It's okay. I don't think we have time. I'm just grabbing a few things, anyway."

I'm pretty sure that lies don't count when the accused was performing good deeds. It might not be in the Bible, but some-where definitely says that.

I rushed toward the building hearing Mom's door shut behind me.

"Geez, where's the fire?"

Her quick steps clipped on the sidewalk behind me and I glanced to see her waving a wet wipe as I climbed the concrete stairs.

I pulled up the tickets on my phone and ducked my head, blocking everything with the sun hat. A bored teenager scanned the tickets as she popped her gum and scrolled videos on her phone.

Nice! Maybe they didn't care about the whole fifty plus thing.

Inside, the building was a breathtaking mixture of old and new. It had large, dark wooden beams and posts, exposed brick walls, old chandeliers, framed newspaper articles, and accents of sleek industrial metal. To the right was a series of rooms, and ahead, a set of stairs and the bathrooms.

"Wow." Mom stopped and stared.

"My thoughts exactly." It was gorgeous.

My mother huffed. "Speaking of gorgeous, you need to wipe that gray off your face and take off that god-awful hat. Is that a bunny on top of it?" Her lips frowned.

The hat was a Savers find. I went with whatever had the biggest brim. The animals and plastic fruit on top of it were a bit much, but taking them off would have ruined more than it helped. "It doesn't matter. I'm not going to see anyone I know. And it's not a bunny...I'm pretty sure it's a mouse?" I waved her off, but then to the right I noticed a KISMET SILVERS EVENT sign on an easel next to the double doors that were propped open.

Shoot. I tried to block the sign with my body as we passed. Mom tipped her head to the side and moved behind me to read the sign.

"What is Kismet Silvers?"

It was too soon—she would bolt.

"No idea." I looked around, desperate for a distraction. Perfect! Bathrooms. "I need to use the bathroom, then we can figure out where the inventory they want to get rid of is." I nodded to the bathrooms off to the left.

She followed me to the restroom and began fluffing her hair and applying her lipstick. I stepped into the stall and carefully went over my plan.

Make sure no one looks at me.

Make Mom find a date.

Preferably a rich date.

When I came out to wash my hands Mom swiped my hat off my head, handed me a wet wipe, and threw my hat into the garbage in a swift ninja-like movement.

"Hey!" I felt where my hat used to be. "I just bought that hat."

"Why?" Mom grimaced.

I straightened. "Um, I thought it looked good on me?" It was a stretch, but I couldn't tell her it was a disguise.

"How much was it?"

"Two dollars..."

Mom rolled her eyes, dug in her purse, grabbed two dollars, and thrust them into my hand. "Consider yourself reimbursed."

She lifted her chin, "I'm sorry dear, it had to be done. I'll buy you a new one. One without an entire farmers market on top of it." She shuddered and nodded at my face and its gray lines and then the wet wipe.

She did not look sorry at all. Hopefully they wouldn't care too much about the fifty and up thing, because this had just gotten much harder.

Mom stepped back, taking in my appearance. The blond hair was now straight against my collar bone, my face had no wrinkle lines, and my knee-length vintage dark blue and white polka-dot dress met with her nod of approval. "You are beautiful, Emma." Mom gave me a quick hug. "Inside and out." Her eyebrows fell. "But that hat, again." She shuddered.

I chuckled. "Fine, let's go see what we can find."

We left the bathroom and headed into the room with the open doors. It smelled like peppermint and a very strong floral perfume.

Large groups of people mingled throughout the room. I

looked at the round table near the entrance, and a woman with a pointy nose and glasses studied her clipboard. "Names." Her nasal voice startled me.

"Hannah Woods and guest." I tried my best to keep my chin tucked and to avoid eye contact. I really hoped I wasn't caught before we even got inside.

I heard the scratching of paper and saw her check Mom's name off the list. She looked quizzically at me as she handed us two name tags, and I looped Mom's elbow in mine and pulled her into the room. Hopefully, if nothing else we could get lost in the crowd.

"Why was it my name on the list and not yours?" Mom asked, as she looked back at the round table.

"Hm." I did my best to ignore the question as I looked for future hiding places.

"Em." She pulled me to a stop, her blue eyes full of questions as she looked around the room. "Why did they have my name and not yours?" Several men nodded in her direction. "It doesn't look like there's inventory they want to get rid of in here. It's like a reception or something." She looked at the front of the room with the stage. "Are we at the wrong place?" She turned toward the front door.

I searched the room, desperate for something to distract her. I nodded to a table piled with desserts toward the back of the room.

"Look, maybe we are in the right place after all."

"Emma! Are you thinking of stealing desserts?" Mom chastised me in a whisper.

"Mom, we're on the list. I think they are for us." I pointed to our name tags.

Mom's lips frowned, but she didn't resist as I pulled us to the table. I picked up two glass plates and handed her one. I went along the white lace tablecloth and grabbed a cookie and a slice of cake. I waited at the end of the table for Mom, and while she was distracted by the desserts, I scanned the room for potential dates.

"What are you looking for?" Mom asked.

"Geez!" I jumped, nearly dropping my plate. "You scared me." I nodded to a table in the back corner. "Want to sit and eat? Then I will see if I can find someone with the inventory."

She nodded. "Sure."

I led us to a table on the edge of the room, trying to recognize faces and attach them to profiles I'd seen. I picked up my cookie and took a bite.

The sound system clicked on, and I looked in horror at the stage and the older gentleman in a suit standing behind a microphone stand. He was about to welcome everyone to the singles event, and the perfect moment for confession hadn't come.

Looked like the jig might be up.

Crap! Crap! Crap! I looked around for some way to kill the power.

Mom looked up from the bite of angel food cake poised in front of her mouth.

"I would like to welcome everyone to the first of many Kismet Silvers events." Applause scattered through the room.

Mom raised her eyebrows.

I admit it, I even considered throwing my high heel shoe, in hopes of knocking out the old man and shutting him up. I looked everywhere but at Mom.

"A safe dating environment for patrons fifty and up," the man continued.

Mom's eyes grew wide.

"I don't know about you, but I have found it hard to meet single people with similar interests and close in age. I started this event hoping we may all find friendships and company in our aging years." He chuckled. "I may be sixty, but I think I still have good years of life to live." He winked at the crowd.

I was so dead.

I fidgeted in my seat.

Mom turned her body to face me, fire blazing in her eyes.

I cleared my throat. "So...how's the cake?"

Chapter Four

"Emma Ann Woods." Mom whisper-yelled each portion of my name. I could see the heat rising on her face.

Shoot.

I was so close.

"I can explain." I held my hands in front of me.

"Get to it." Her body was rigid.

My shoulders tensed—actually, I couldn't explain. I'd thought of this moment over and over and was banking on something coming to me.

It didn't come.

"Emma." She growled

Looked like the truth was all I had. I sighed. "I was looking at this dating app thing and there was an ad for Kismet Silvers. It's for fifty and up and has all sorts of activities. It looked like a blast, but I thought you wouldn't come if you knew it was for dating."

"You thought right," she looked to the exit.

"Mom, come on. Just try it out..."

"Absolutely not." Mom crossed her arms and her lips pinched in anger. "We're leaving right now." Her eyebrow raised, daring me to challenge her decision. "Wait." She tipped her head back and closed her eyes. "Do you even need help at your apartment tonight?" Her blue eyes met mine, hope barely visible.

I dipped my shoulders and shook my head.

"Wow, Em."

I couldn't look her in the eyes, but I had come too far to give up now. "Just give me fifteen minutes. You sit here and eat dessert."

She eyed her plate of dessert. "To do what, exactly?"

"See if any of these men would take you to Europe or if they have horses?"

"What are you talking about?" Mom pinched the bridge of her nose as each word came out with more exhaustion than the last.

"Some of these guys have horse ranches and Ferraris." I nodded my head toward the crowds mingling about. "I'm sure of it."

She leaned on her fist and raised a brow. "Yeah, and some have mounds of debt, broods of kids and grandkids, and expectations of what a wife should be." Mom rolled her eyes. "I'm done, Em. If you won't take me home, I'll call Betty."

My stomach sank as I watched her dig in her purse for her phone. When she found out it wouldn't work, it would be spray-painted Spike all over again. Probably worse. Well, so much for making sure no one saw me.

"I'll be right back." She would forgive me later...hopefully. I bolted, nearly causing my chair to fly back.

I opened the notes on my phone and walked between the tables and eavesdropped on conversations.

Fred was divorced and desperate.

Fred—No.

Hank grumbled about collection calls.

Hank—No.

Charlie mentioned a medical procedure accompanied by buckets of oozing pus.

Yikes!

Charlie—No.

This was less promising than I'd hoped. I looked around the room.

On the back wall, beside a large window, stood a George Clooney look-alike talking with a group of gentlemen whose appearance screamed *I have a yacht and a red Ferrari*. Tailored suits, flashy watches, a golf club exclusive type stance. The GC look-alike had on black slacks and a pressed striped button-up shirt. He flashed gold jewelry and a smile.

Mom waved her hand, catching my attention, and then pointed to her phone.

I acted like I didn't know what she meant, and picked up speed toward my target. GC2 scowled at me, but continued the conversation about his new sailboat. I refrained from giving a fist bump. Called it!

Mom would love to sail.

After hearing his dark velvety voice and seeing him, I remembered he was the man who welcomed us to the event. Should I still ask him?

It would be a risk, but he still might be my best option.

He had a sailboat.

I pursed my lips and twisted slightly on my high heels. How would I ask him on a date for Mom and not sound super creepy?

"Excuse me, can I help you?" GC2 turned to me, giving me a full view of his name tag. Darian Cole.

"Sorry, I didn't want to interrupt." I cringed. "I...I just thought I heard you mention a boat?" Why was my voice so high? I cleared my throat.

"Yes." The man's tone was hesitant.

"Can I ask what kind?" I did my best to be sweet.

"Why does it matter?" His mouth pulled down into a frown.

Yikes. "I was only making small talk, because well..." I stopped before I mentioned Mom. "I was thinking of owning a boat myself."

The man shot a puzzled look at the other gentlemen. "You

don't look fifty." Darian Cole folded his arms and glared down his long nose at me.

"Oh, that's because I..." I almost said I wasn't, but the man narrowed his eyes in anger. I decided not to mention my age.

Abort mission. Something about this man had danger warning alarms going off in my mind.

"Um...I have a great doctor." I turned away. "Enjoy your evening." I scurried away to a corner.

That man... Well, he was terrifying. It took all I had not to turn and see if he was still watching me. I shook off the negative vibes that still reached out to me.

I tried to slow my breathing as I opened my notes and typed *Darian Cole—NO!!*

I didn't want this night to be a total loss. What else could I try? I met Mom's eyes, and she snapped her finger and pointed to the table. I knew that from my childhood this meant time was up. I had pushed my luck as far as it would stretch.

An older man with a cane blocked my path. He smiled at me with a gap-toothed grin as I glanced at him curiously.

He wasn't my first choice, but maybe he had horses?

"Good evening." I nodded.

"Hello there, Miss." The man raised his eyebrows. "With shoes like those, your feet must have great arches." He grinned. His eyes roamed down my legs and landed on my feet. "Can I look at them?"

Wait. What?

"Your feet." He gestured toward them again.

"You want to look at my feet?" What was he talking about? I shook my head and figured I must have heard him wrong.

"Oh yes, without your shoes, please." The man looked at my face again, before he rubbed his hands together in anticipation as he practically drooled.

Ew! Gross!

I checked the name tag. Brad.

I ran away and held back the gagging sound in my throat. I opened my notepad on my phone.

Brad—NO NO NO.

What a waste. Time to admit defeat, beg forgiveness, and go home.

I peeked over my shoulder and saw the man with the cane in slow but steady pursuit. For the first time in my life, I might agree with Jane that running had some sudden new benefits.

I glanced at the table where I'd left Mom. She was talking to another woman beside her and smiled. I couldn't leave now. Maybe I could hide? I continued through the room while keeping my eyes on Mom.

Mom's eyes met mine and her eyebrows suddenly pulled down in concern, then I slammed into something solid. My nose smashed against an immovable wall of muscle, and my phone went flying. I stumbled back.

My eyes watered as I reached up and gingerly pressed around my nose.

Ouch!

Apparently, I'd hit a man. What the heck was this guy made of? Concrete? My gaze followed the shoes upward.

Oh wow.

My mouth fell open. Maybe it was because I'd spent the evening pinballing between fifty-year-old men, or maybe my vision was still blurry, but holy hot cakes... wow. He looked vaguely familiar, but surely I would have remembered him.

The man had sharp brown eyes and tightly trimmed facial hair. He towered over me in suit pants and a long sleeve button-up shirt snug against his chest. My throat tightened. He smelled divine, like the smell of rain after a dry spell. I was drawn to him, pulled in by his magnetism.

His lip dropped into a grimace and his eyes fell to my phone lying face-up on his shoe, screen glowing with my long list of NOs.

Whoops!

I bent and scooped up the phone. "I'm so sorry! I wasn't watching where I was walking and—"

"Age?" His voice was a low grumble.

I checked his finger. No ring. Not that it mattered...

Wait. "What was that?"

"How old are you?" Mr. Muscles asked, his voice clipped. "Also, I need you to delete whatever information you collected tonight." He gestured toward my phone.

My forehead wrinkled. "What?"

"Now," he said firmly, holding out his hand.

Okay, hot and rude!

I smiled smugly and dropped the phone into my purse. Not happening.

Mr. Muscles raised an eyebrow, clearly unimpressed. He didn't move. He just stood there, a Greek god statue brought to life. "Were you aware you needed to be over fifty to attend any of these events?" His facial expression was cold.

"You're one to talk." I shot right back, planting my hand on my hip.

He dipped his head condescending, arms folded over his perfect chest. I wondered if he ever popped a button that way.

"You need to leave. Now."

I had planned on leaving, but now I didn't want this guy to tell me what to do. Then GC2 walked up and stood beside him, and those creepy vibes reached out for me again. I was not messing with that guy.

Fine.

I sighed and turned to get Mom when a large firm hand dropped on my shoulder. "Not that way," Mr. Muscles rumbled.

I scoffed, shaking off his grip—my shoulder still feeling warm from where his touch had been. Annoying.

"As owner of this establishment," he practically growled, "and as part of my contract with Kismet Silvers," he nodded to Darian Cole, "no one under the age of fifty is allowed at these events." His eyebrow slowly raised. "There have been problems with gold diggers before."

Gross.

"What?" I squeaked. "I am not a gold digger!"

"Your notes and complaints tonight would say otherwise." The arrogant man cleared his throat. "Now, would you like for me to send for security? Because I can."

Please, like it would take more than him to muscle me out of here.

I was so annoyed. The entire room stared at me, and I felt the anger and embarrassment of the attention burning my face.

"That won't be necessary." I added in my fakest sugary tone and stepped away from him. "I'm leaving."

A hand grabbed my arm at my side, and I jumped to see Mom standing beside me.

"We're both leaving." Mom glared at the man, obviously not intimidated by his size. She wrapped her arm through my elbow.

The man stepped to the side, motioning for us to continue. Mr. Cole grabbed onto Muscles and began whisper-yelling something to him.

"You better fix my phone," she chastised me under her breath as we walked toward the exit.

What a horrible man! If I never saw him again, it would still be too soon.

Chapter Five

MOM "CORRECTED" ME FOR AN HOUR ON HOW IT WASN'T
my place to trick her into dating, and how important honesty was
between us. I agreed to cancel her Kismet Silvers account, and I got
on the next day to do just that. But...I accidentally clicked the
events tab, and the next week's activity felt too serendipitous. It
was a night about world travel. There were dance lessons, raffles for
tons of things, including a trip to Spain, classes to make noodles...
If anything screamed happiness for my mother, it was this.

I flipped the frustrating hair out of my face as I set my phone
on the checkout counter at The Bees Knees.

My stomach had been riding a roller coaster of nausea ever
since I purchased the ticket and raffle vouchers three days ago for
the Kismet Silvers site. I changed the flyer to remove Kismet
Singles and sent them to Mom for a exclusive world travel event
from a fake email.

Every day, I wondered if it would be the day she would call,
either to invite me to join her or to call and say she hated me and
never wanted to talk to me again.

So far still nothing.

I wasn't sure which option I preferred, although I knew which one I deserved.

I rubbed my forehead with my left hand and tried to force myself to swallow through the lump in my throat as I adjusted my navy blue polka dot top.

This cupid stuff had quickly spiraled out of hand. Once I got an idea, I had always struggled to let go. Part of me begged to stop, but I ignored it anyway. I rubbed my temples and the headache forming there.

The bell sounded over the door, and Jane walked in holding a green smoothie. "Why are *you* upset? I'm the one you stood up for a double date on Friday."

I sighed. "I didn't stand you up. I told you I wouldn't be going." I raised my hands. "How is any of that standing you up?"

Jane waved me off. "Semantics. You knew I wanted you to come."

"True." I needed to get busy or Jane would catch on that I had not canceled Mom's account when I said I did. Since I was little, she could sniff out my lies like a bloodhound. I picked up a jar of the penny candy and went around the counter to try to stock the already full jars. Jane put her hands on the counter behind her and jumped up and sat on it.

"You could have a date this weekend if you used the app for yourself instead of your mom." Jane eyed me with her brows raised.

"Maybe yes, maybe no." I moved the jar to my other hand and looked anywhere but Jane's eyes.

"Has your mom forgiven you yet?" Jane sipped on her weird green drink.

I'd told Jane everything about that night, although I should have mentioned fewer muscles on the boss guy. Time to change the subject. "How's it going with Finn?"

She pinched her lips. "Not great." She shook her head. "Some-times things seem great between us, then he will pretend like he doesn't even know me." She raised her brows. "Don't go getting any ideas. It's my turn to set you up. And this time you can't cancel last minute."

"Oh. Um, I..." My stomach churned. Could I say no after I set up other people all the time, including her?

Jane raised an eyebrow. "Why not? Not as fun when you're not the one shooting Cupid's arrow?" She frowned. "Or do you not trust my judgement to get you a date?"

I rolled my eyes and put the jar of green apple sugar sticks back. "You can always find a date. The problem is they might expect your friends to look like you." I nodded to Jane. She was the modern man's dream—lean muscle, health fanatic, modern fashion, tan clear skin, and legs for days.

"What does that mean?" Jane spun around to face me on the other side of the counter as she finished her green smoothie.

"Oh, come on." I gestured toward her and then to me. "We aren't exactly the same pants size." I didn't mind my comfort curves, but I didn't want to be in direct comparison with her either.

She shook her head. "You're gorgeous, Em. If they don't see it, it's on them."

"I didn't say it wouldn't be, but also..." I flinched and grabbed the assorted flavored honey and went around the counter. "I don't blind date well. I'm more of an acquired taste, but then people's taste buds seem to change."

"It would help if you didn't expect your dates to appear in black and white." Jane hopped off the counter and threw away her paper cup.

"I don't expect them to be from the 1950s." I rolled my eyes. "I would also be okay with the 1920s." I grinned.

Jane grabbed a jar of hard candies and set it on the counter. I traded her the honey sticks, and she picked them up, setting them back on the shelf. "I'm serious, Em. You will never find love if you don't stop running."

I nodded in acknowledgment. "Fair."

Jane straightened the jars on the shelf so the labels faced forward, and then she turned to look at me, her thin frame full of frustration. "Why won't you at least try?"

I sighed and raised a shoulder. "Finding a good fit with dating just feels impossible sometimes."

She put her hands on her hips. "What does Audrey Hepburn say about something being impossible?" She waited.

I chuckled.

She held out her hand and gestured for me to answer.

"Nothing is impossible, the word itself says *I'm possible*."

"Exactly." Jane nodded. "Oh, I know!" She clapped and rushed over to me. "I should go see if I can find that angry Mr. Muscles." She wiggled her eyebrows. "From the way you describe him, he would have no problem sweeping you off your feet."

"Stop!" I smiled as I raised my hands. "Mr. Muscles is eye candy best enjoyed from a distance."

She nodded. "Plus, seeing him might be harder now that you canceled your mom's account and won't be at his venue."

"Yep." I internally flinched at the lie. I wiped imaginary dust off the counter. It wasn't a complete lie. I had every intention of not letting him see me at the next event.

My phone vibrated on the counter, and Mom's face lit up the screen.

I'd been waiting for this call for days, and of course she called right now. I reached over and silenced the call.

Jane shot me a questioning glance.

I avoided eye contact. "I'll call her back after you leave." If I tried to talk to Mom while she was here, there was no way Jane wouldn't find out.

The phone vibrated again.

Not now, Mom!

I rushed forward and silenced it. I could feel the sweat gathering in my palms.

"It's rude to not answer your mother. What if she needs you?" Jane eyed me suspiciously.

The phone started to ring again, and Jane rushed at it before I could hit ignore.

Crap!

"Hey, Hannah! Were you wanting to talk to Em?" Jane grinned and listened.

What was Mom going to tell her?

"Yeah, I heard about that." Jane shook her head.

I held my hand out for the phone, hoping to prevent the inevitable. Jane swatted my hand away and stepped toward the furniture section.

I hurried after her and reached desperately for the phone. Jane's height and exercise habits both worked to her advantage.

Jane stopped. "Wait. You got what in an email?" She slowly turned to me.

I stopped chasing and waited for my punishment.

"I see." There was a long, drawn-out silence. "Therapy," Jane mouthed to me.

I dropped into a nearby chair as Jane glared daggers at me.

I was a terrible daughter and friend.

"You're right, she owes you." She raised her right eyebrow. "More than you know. Here, I will let you talk to Em." Jane hit the mute button.

"Seriously, Em! After you told her you wouldn't?" Her lips pinched, and her hand shook as she held out the phone for me to take. "I can't even right now!" She slapped the phone into my palm. "You better tell her the truth. If you trick her again…" She stalked off to the front door and pushed it harder than necessary.

I flinched as the bell above the door held on for dear life.

I sighed and hit the unmute button. "Hey, Mom." My voice was falsely chipper.

I SAT IN MY YELLOW BUG ON THE LONG GRAVEL driveway of Mom's farmhouse, hating myself for being a terrible daughter. Logic told me to come clean. Logic told me not to go. I guess logic wasn't loud enough.

I should have done so many things differently. But there I sat, waiting to take Mom to tonight's Kismet Silvers event, against her knowledge.

Mom would love the world travel event, I rationalized. But by the sinking of my stomach I knew that Jane was right. Maybe all this "noble cupid stuff" wasn't for my mom at all.

I pressed my forehead against the steering wheel, my blond curls falling around my face. My hands were warm and sticky.

I could still cancel.

Mom's front door opened, and she stepped out of her house wearing a black and red Spanish-style dress and a huge smile.

She looked beautiful. I was a horrible daughter.

Mom pulled open the car door. "Thanks for coming with me tonight, Em," Mom said, sliding in and clicking her seat belt. "I figured you owed me after last week." She teased cheerfully.

She had no idea.

She was too good. I put the car into reverse and backed out of the driveway.

"Do you need the address?" Mom clicked on her phone.

My guilt burned higher up my throat. I had changed the address when I erased any trace of Kismet Singles on the flyer, another way I'd lied to Mom. I couldn't look at her face.

"Nope, you texted it to me earlier." I used a different route to The Brick House. "So how's Ivy been feeling?" I knew if I needed Mom to fill the silence, all I had to do was ask about her kids. Even though I was just postponing the inevitable.

Maybe like dating, I was avoiding pain and trying to take an easier route.

The drive passed with stories of Bunco night, her long hours at work, and a new kitchen gadget that she decided she needed but couldn't figure out how to use.

I turned on my blinker and pulled into the parking lot. I found a parking spot and cut the engine, waiting for Mom to realize where she was.

She looked over her shoulder. "You got the address wrong, let me check again." She flipped the flyer open and then paused. "Wait…" She glanced in confusion between the flyer, the building, and me.

I dropped my head to the steering wheel.

"You didn't… Did you?" Her voice was a broken whisper.

I shook my head as I placed it into my hands. "Mom…I'm so sorry."

"You did this." Mom whispered as she stared at the flyer, the hurt evident in her slouched shoulders and quiet voice.

Mom didn't yell. She didn't storm out. She just…sank into her seat, shaking her head. Somehow, that was worse. The anger I could have handled. The disappointment? That crushed me.

"All the information about the event and raffle tickets is accurate. It's also a Kismet Silvers event, and yes I emailed you the information and tickets."

"Why?" she whispered. Her sad blue eyes met mine. "Why didn't you listen?"

I broke eye contact and winced. "I signed on to cancel your account, like you asked." I stared at my car ceiling, tears on my cheeks. "But there was this event and it just seemed too perfect… I knew logically I shouldn't, but I did it anyway."

How had I let it get this far? I wasn't just meddling anymore—I was manipulating. I hated myself for it, and yet, somehow, I had convinced myself it was okay. That it was for her. Mom looked out the window toward the building and dug in her purse.

I felt ugly from head to toe. I grabbed a tissue from Mom's extended hand and blew my nose. The tears flowed freely now that I had let them escape.

Grabbing my phone, I brought up the Kismet website. "Here. I will delete it." I showed Mom as I clicked the deactivate button on her account.

I glanced tentatively at her. "I will never do anything like this again." Her bright face from earlier had lost its glow. "No more tricks." I rubbed my forehead. "I can take you home, or I can come in with you."

We sat in silence. Mom looked from The Brick House to me, and I gave her space to decide what she wanted.

Mom exhaled slowly, her fingers tracing the edge of the flyer. "I don't know." She looked at the building again, then at me, eyes unreadable. "I'm still so mad at you."

"I know."

"Is there really a chance to win a trip to Spain?" She pinched her nose with her thumb and forefinger.

"Yeah. They have a bunch of themed rooms of different locations and each has prizes." I wiped errant tears with the palms of my hands. "I think you could love it, but wish I had just called and talked to you about it instead."

She pinched her lips. "To make it up to me, you will go on a date with the next person who asks, and you will give it a chance." She raised her brows, challenging me to refuse.

I nodded in defeat. "Sure. That's fair."

"No. That's not even close to fair." She pointed at me. "There will be more."

"Yep. Okay." I nodded.

Silence stretched between us as I waited for her decision.

She let out a long sigh. "Fine. But only because I want to use these tickets. And you owe me."

I nodded.

"And Em..."

I looked at her blue eyes.

"Never again."

"Never again," I repeated and I meant it with every part of me.

"And...I'm not here to date."

I nodded, I didn't even care about her dating anymore. I just didn't want her upset with me.

"And you are coming in with me to see me waste all your money," she said with a sassy grin.

"Okay." I grabbed my ball cap from the back seat, and climbed out of the car. Walking to the other side, I threaded my arm through Mom's elbow and rested my head on her shoulder.

"I don't deserve you," I whispered.

"It's true." She bumped into me. "Not your proudest moment."

I nodded in agreement. "Very true," I acknowledged. I saw the teenager poised in front of the doors again, scanning tickets. "Um, in the spirit of being honest. It says I have to be over fifty to come in." I pressed my lips together and flinched a little.

Mom stopped walking and turned to meet my eyes. "The makeup from before..."

"Yep," I said, nodding and then pointing to the hat, "and the hat..." I placed it on my head.

She sighed. "Well, I guess you will just have to figure it out," she muttered under her breath. "I will give it to you. You're nothing if not creative."

Luckily the same teen couldn't care less as she scanned our tickets.

Now I just had to not get caught by Mr. Muscles or Darian Cole.

I tugged my hat down and looped my arm through Mom's, focused on keeping my head lowered.

Chapter Six

ONCE INSIDE, I HELPED MOM OUT OF HER JACKET AND hung it up. My blue A-Line skirt clung to my knees from the static. "All right, where to, boss?" I grabbed and shook out my skirt.

She tipped her head toward me. "So is it true the rooms are themed as different places?" she asked.

"Yep. There should be a few raffles associated with each location too. Like Italy had wine tasting and a cooking class. I think there was a Latin dance class in Spain."

She fanned out the raffle tickets like a deck of cards. "Please tell me these weren't cheap."

I chuckled and shook my head. "Oh no, they were not cheap." I had spent several hundred dollars on the raffle tickets alone, clearing out more of my bank account than I should have. Probably another result of my guilty conscience.

Mom looked between the two rooms on the main level and the stairs, her lips pinched. "I'm not sure where to start."

"Europe has great desserts." I shrugged.

Mom smiled. "Oh, I bet you're right."

"Looks like Europe is upstairs and to the left." I said, looking at the sign posted at the bottom of the stairs.

She grabbed my hand and led me up the stairs. I kept my face tilted as low as I could without falling.

At the top of the stairs, Europe was to the left and Africa to the right.

We stepped into a dimly lit room draped in soft white curtains with little round tables and an accordion player in the corner. The room was elegant and romantic. Mom's eyes sparkled. "This is gorgeous, Em!"

I gave her a soft smile. "Dessert or raffle tickets first?"

"Let's waste your hard-earned money first." She winked at me and led me through the room, her Spanish skirt swishing as we made our way to a set of long tables with large glass containers and descriptions of each raffle item. Cooking classes, dancing classes, language lessons, wine, and weekend trips. Mom put several of her tickets into the jars. I hoped she'd win something; she deserved it.

"Dessert?" She squeezed my hand.

"Always."

She led us to the dessert tables and grabbed two small plates, handing one of them to me. After grabbing some pastries, I followed her to a lace-covered table with a candle and a vase with fresh flowers set in the middle. People mingled in groups of five or six, adding a soft murmur throughout the room.

She picked up a small chocolate pastry, put it in her mouth, and sighed. "Absolutely divine."

I followed suit. I would be more than happy to sit at this table and watch Mom have fun, but I didn't mind the mini desserts either.

I took another bite of my tartlet. "If you win the pasta one, can I come? That sounds so fun."

Mom scowled. "No, I think as punishment, you can't come to anything I win." She placed her hands on her hips.

I nodded. "Fair."

"Hannah?"

I jumped at the male voice behind me and covered my face.

"Hannah Peters, is that you?"

"Robert?"

I watched as Mom gasped, lips parting. She rushed over, giving the stranger a hug.

"Gosh, it's been ages. How are you?"

I hadn't heard anyone call her by her maiden name before, and I had never seen her blush like that.

Robert held Mom's shoulders and smiled down at her, awestruck. "I'm well enough. And you?"

"I'm good."

"It's so good to see you." Robert grinned and looked into Mom's eyes. Robert had gray hair, blue eyes, a large smile, and square jawline.

Oh my gosh! This was actually happening. I tried to stop my feet from stamping in excitement and was unsuccessful.

Don't meddle... Don't meddle.

I bit back my smile and stood. Maybe I could sneak away and give them some privacy. I set my plate on a tray and went to slip out.

Looking toward the doorway, an angry Greek god with a pair of frustrated brown eyes met mine.

Crap! I flinched and ducked my face behind my cap. Not him again!

I turned back to see Mom sitting at the table, now with Robert by her side, laughing at something he said.

No way I was breaking that up. I made a quick decision to run for it.

Ok, not run. I was in heels, after all. I didn't even run in tennis shoes.

Weaving through people and tables, I made my way deeper into the room.

Maybe I could find another exit? There was nothing but walls and windows, and the windows wouldn't open. I'm not sure what I would have done if they did.

Ugh!

I stood behind a wooden pillar and peeked toward the door. Muscles wasn't looking in my direction.

Now, if I could wait for the opportune moment. Just then, a man with a cane grabbed Muscles' arm and pulled his attention down to him.

Now!

I crouched down and scurried to the curtains on the side of the wall. If I could make it to the group of tables holding raffle items, I could hide behind them.

I slipped behind a group of women, then dove behind the tables. Hard carpet met my knees.

Ow. My knees heated and burned.

The table was close enough to the wall that I could shimmy between it and the wall on hands and knees to the end of the table. I snuck out from under the tablecloth. There was still a good six to ten feet to the exit and no tables left to block my path. I eased around the corner to check on Muscles, but I couldn't see anything from that angle. I crouched higher, looking out from behind a tiered tray of cupcakes.

Found him. He was at the back of the room.

I could make it!

I bolted for the door, my eyes focused on Muscles. Unfortunately for me and the woman in the muumuu dress I nearly tackled, I was not watching where I was going. The lady threw her hands in the air, sending her Mary Poppins bag flying in an explosion of tissues, medicine, peppermint candies, and cracker packs. Her arms waved desperately as she tried to steady herself.

"I'm so sorry!" I reached for her and held her steady. "Are you okay? Did I hurt you?" I checked her up and down for emerging bruises.

"Oh, it's fine." The woman gave me a sweet smile as she released her grip on my arms. "That sure works to jump-start the ticker though." She chuckled, placing a hand on her heart.

"I'm so sorry I wasn't watching where I was going." I wrapped my arm around her. "Here. Let me help you sit, and then I will get your bag." I led her to the first empty chair. Once she was sitting, I bent down to see her eyes. "Are you sure you are okay?"

"Yes, dearie. I'm fine." She placed her warm hand on my cheek.

I smiled, glad she wasn't showing signs of a heart attack. I returned to the Mary Poppins bag and began the hunt for peppermint candies and Advil. Scooping up the items, I was surprised at the distance some things flew. I took a last look around.

There!

The last package of crackers was a few feet away, and I bent down, but before I grabbed it, another large hand picked it up. I looked up to a set of fiery brown eyes and muttered a curse under my breath.

He smirked. "My thoughts exactly."

I rolled my eyes. "At least let me return her bag first." I didn't wait for his answer as I grabbed the crackers out of his hands, my fingertips trailing along his palm. I returned the bag and apologized once again.

I looked between Muscles and the door. There would be no outrunning him now.

"I really didn't expect to see you again," he growled, and brought my attention back to his trimmed beard and wavy brown hair.

"I had hoped you wouldn't see me too," I replied with a grin.

His lips pulled down in a frown. "That is not what I said."

I waved him off. "Let me guess. I can leave or you will call security." I raised an eyebrow.

Muscles nodded.

"Figured." I shrugged. "Let me get my mom."

His forehead wrinkled in confusion. "You're here with your mom?"

I tipped my head, "Yeah, she was with me last time too." I side-eyed him. "Don't you remember? She walked out with me..." I made my way farther into the room.

His scowl deepened, "Honestly no, I remembered someone being beside you, but I didn't really look at who." He paused. "It was a very long day." His voice lost some of its edge and I didn't push. I headed toward the table where Mom sat. She reached over and patted Robert's arm.

Dang. I wish I didn't have to cut this short.

"Hey, Mom, sorry to interrupt," I smiled at Robert, "but I guess we're leaving." I motioned my head to Mr. Muscles looming over my shoulder.

Mom leaned and looked at the man behind me. She grinned. "No thanks."

"What?" My eyes opened wide.

"I think I am going to stay until the drawing of the raffles, in case I win something." She motioned for Muscles to come closer with her hand. "Excuse me, can you help me?" Mom met my eyes and mouthed, "My turn."

Wait, what?

I stepped back and felt the warmth of Muscles' chest close behind me.

Whoa!

"That's fine. Text me when you are ready for a ride. I'll be nearby." I had no desire to break up the reunion between Mom and her friend anyway.

"How can I help you?" Muscles' voice was full of caution.

"Well, you see, my phone battery has died." She lifted her phone and shook it dramatically in the air. "Now, I know my daughter isn't supposed to be here," she shook her head at me with a look of shame, "but she can't leave or I won't have a ride home." Mom's lips formed a slight pout.

Really, Mom? I quirked a brow.

"It's okay, Hannah," Robert spoke up. "I would be happy to give you a—"

A distinct thump came from under the table, followed by a look of pain and confusion on Robert's face. I coughed to cover my laugh.

Mom looked at Muscles before flashing her grip of raffle tickets. "I purchased all these raffle tickets, and as a paying customer, I'm sure you're okay with my daughter waiting in the foyer for me, just so I can see if I win anything. Right?"

"I'm not sure that is a good idea..." Muscles' voice had changed, the hard edge melted just a fraction. I peeked up at him over my shoulder. His lips were in a straight line.

"What if she doesn't talk to anyone attending the party?" she continued to beg. "Just so I can have a ride home? I'm sure you'd want your mother to be treated kindly as well."

Wow, she was good.

Mom tapped her chin. "I know!" She smiled. "You could stay with her and make sure she obeys the rules."

Muscles shifted beside me.

Okay, game over.

I was not being babysat by a grown man. "I will be in the car." I waved goodbye to mom.

"Come, now," Mom called. "You will freeze, and I know you." She raised a brow. "You'll starve."

I gasped. "Mom!"

Muscles cleared his throat in what was surely an attempt to hide a laugh.

"I can just start the car if I get cold. It's fine." I turned to leave.

Mom tsked. "I'm sure the ozone layer would not approve. It's everyone's job to care for the Earth. Surely you'd rather sit patiently where it was warm and bright rather than irreparably ruin the environment, dear." Her lips pinched down in a frown as she shook her head.

If Muscles wanted to stay and listen to Mom he could, but I was leaving. "Let me know when you are ready, Mom. I'm sure you will find a way. After all, you're nothing if not creative." I grinned back at her as I walked toward the exit. I passed the dessert table and snagged a chocolate cupcake for the road.

No need to be cold *and* hungry.

Chapter Seven

I grabbed my jacket and headed out the front doors and down the steps. The cool night air was a welcome relief. Despite everything, the evening was a success. Mom had reconnected with an old friend, and I scored a cupcake—I took a victory bite. I was still swearing off lying for the sake of Cupid. That was bad.

"Wait," a deep male voice called behind me.

I jumped and nearly choked on my cupcake. I spun around to see Mr. Muscles standing there, brown eyes locked on me with a lopsided grin.

"What?" I coughed, my hand over my mouth that was still half-full. "I'm outside." I gestured to the parking lot behind me.

He stared at the remaining half of my cupcake.

Oh no! He was not taking my cupcake too. Before he could make a move, I stuffed the rest into my mouth in one defiant bite, while keeping eye contact.

His grin widened, revealing a dimple on his left cheek. His smile was sweet, and he looked like a different man from before, the dimple giving me déjà vu. "Your mother might be right; you could be starving."

I swallowed, the cake coating my throat and changing my voice two octaves lower. "I can come back when my mom's done." I cleared my throat and ran my tongue along my teeth covered behind my hand and repeated. "I can come back when Mom's done."

He grinned. "Her phone is dead though, remember?"

Very unlikely.

"Truuee." I drew out the word. "I'll wait in the car then."

He motioned with his head for me to follow him. "Come back inside."

I looked over my shoulder through the parking lot. "I thought I wasn't supposed to be in there."

"Oh you aren't," he said with a smile. "But if I make sure you aren't harassing anyone, it should be fine..." Muscles' casual expression changed. "But just for tonight. I really need to attempt to keep Mr. Cole happy." His forehead creased.

I scoffed. "I never harassed anyone."

"Debatable." He chuckled as he held the door open for me. "It's warmer inside." He gestured toward the foyer.

I hesitantly walked up a few steps. "You're sure you want me to come inside?" Where was the grumpy scowling man from before?

"I do." He nodded.

I watched his eyes, waiting for the magic spell to wear off as I slowly stepped into the building.

"May I hang up your coat?" he asked, reaching for my jacket.

I stepped back. "Okay, hold up. Who are you? And where is the man from before?" I tipped my head to the side.

He ran a hand through his brown hair. "I might have overreacted last time." He shrugged. "This event's success is paramount for The Brick House, and Cole gets under my skin."

I eyed him with skepticism, although I could admit that the danger vibes I felt had come from the older man. There was something about the way Muscles ran his hand through his hair that was so familiar.

He looked down at my eyes, holding contact. "I haven't been at my best. I'm sorry." He sighed. "It's been a very long few months." He held his hand out between us. "Let's start over. My name is Grant."

"Grant?" My eyebrows lowered, but I held out my hand. "As in Cary Grant?"

His forehead wrinkled. "Not sure. I didn't pick it."

What are the odds?

It would be creepy to say I wished for a Grant, right?

Right.

"I'm Emma." I shook his hand. I ignored that my hand tingled from his touch.

"Guess both our parents preferred traditional names." He gestured to a sitting area by the large glass windows.

I walked over to one of the armchairs and sat. Grant followed, sitting in a chair next to mine.

"Were you here before because your mom wanted you to be?"

I flinched. "Um, kinda?"

"Wait." He held his hands up. "You were looking for a date last time?"

"Not for me. Gross. No!" I shuddered.

"I'm not following." Grant eased back in the chair, placing his right elbow on the arm of the chair.

"It's kind of a long story…" I warned him.

He looked at his watch. "Well it looks like you have my attention for the next…twenty-five minutes." He nodded for me to continue. "I'm all ears."

I grimaced. "It's not my 'proudest moment.'" I used air quotes around the words Mom used earlier.

He chuckled. "Perfect. That's what I need right now." He visibly relaxed his shoulders. My breath caught in my throat. He was gorgeous.

"REMIND ME TO NOT GET IN YOUR WAY WHEN YOU ARE determined." He chuckled, then pointed to my rug-burned knees. "What happened there?"

I grimaced. "I might have dived behind the raffle table in an attempt to escape you." I scrunched my nose remembering the failed attempt.

He tipped his head back with a loud, carefree laugh. "I could not figure out how you got past me."

His laugh was rich and deep, and I wanted to wrap its warmth around me. He was hot before, but to watch him now without the stiff exterior and his soft smile, I was in awe.

"I still can't believe you thought I was a gold digger. I wouldn't date someone old enough to be my father." I shuddered. "Well, I'm assuming they are old enough to be my father. I didn't know mine. He left when I was one."

Grant's shoulders stiffened. "Sorry about your dad."

"Don't be." I shrugged. "I don't remember him, so I can't miss him."

Grant stared at the floor. "My father passed a few years ago." His jaw clenched. "I wish I didn't remember him." Whatever his relationship with his dad, I was definitely not getting happy-go-lucky vibes.

I tipped my head and watched him as tense air seemed to be pressing down on him. I raised my hand for a high-five. "No-dad club?"

It was crass, but it worked. He rolled his eyes and gave me a soft high-five.

"You don't have to sit with me. I won't bother anyone." I crossed my heart. "I'm sure you are busy."

"I'm pretty sure my staying with you is in everyone's best inter-est." He shook his head. "You terrified Mr. Hanen last time." He flashed me his dimple with his carefree smile. The man needed a permit to be flashing it about, it was so disarming.

I looked up to the ceiling trying to remember Mr. Hanen and stop gawking at Grant. "Was he the one who asked to see my feet?"

Grant's eyes pulled wide. "Someone asked to see your feet?"

I tried to stop the giggle. "Yep. Like my bare feet." I mimicked vomiting.

"Huh." He shook his head. One corner of his lips pulled up in a mischievous grin. "So, did you show him your feet?"

"Gross! No!" I swatted him on the shoulder.

"Just checking." He laughed.

"Okay, it's your turn." I tucked my hair behind an ear and crossed my ankles.

"My turn to what?"

"Tell me about you." I gestured for him to talk.

Grant leaned back and rubbed his hand through his trimmed beard. "Hmm, okay. Let me think." He tipped his head back. "I have spent far too much time and energy trying to get this business off the ground. I like hard eighties rock like Metallica and AC/DC, salt over sugar," he paused, "and I have never been called a gold digger." His lips split into a wide grin, pleased at his joke.

I rolled my eyes.

Wait...

"You like salt over sugar?!" I shook my head in mock sadness. "What kind of monster are you? We can never be friends now." I held my hand to my heart.

"I think it could work." Grant shrugged. "I get to eat all the salty and you all the sweet. Seems better that way, then we don't have to share." He smiled.

My mouth dropped open. "Huh?" My mind blanked. "I never thought of it that way."

Grant raised his eyebrows. "See, maybe we could be friends after all." He winked and folded his hands behind his head and leaned back, closing his eyes. Effectively straining the sleeves of his button-up shirt against his biceps. He obviously left out the part about the gym, I enjoyed the view of his arms as he relaxed.

"Mr. Kelly?"

I startled at an angry voice behind me. I turned and saw Darian Cole, mouth clenched tight and anger radiating off him in waves.

"Mr. Cole," Grant stood. His back was ramrod straight as he stepped toward him, holding out his hand for a firm handshake. "Good to see you this evening." All the calm that possessed Grant leaked out of him and he was replaced by something colder and less personable.

The older man returned the handshake, and unless I was mistaken, Cole seemed to tighten his grip as hard as possible.

Grant didn't flinch.

"I thought we had an understanding?" Mr. Cole gestured in my direction.

I blushed and looked away.

Grant nodded. "Mr. Cole, this is Emma Woods; she is waiting to give her mother a ride home." Grant gestured to me. "Emma, this is Mr. Darian Cole. He is the man who owns Kismet Silvers." Grant's voice was icy.

I wasn't sure what had shifted in him, but I didn't like it.

I cleared my throat, "Nice to meet you...again." I held my hand out to him. Would he squeeze my hand like he had Grant's?

Mr. Cole scowled at me, ignoring my hand, and then shifted his gaze to Grant. "Mr. Kelly, we have a contract and I expect it to be upheld. The only reason I haven't pulled my contract is out of respect for your late father and our friendship."

Grant nodded. "Understood. I assure you. I'm aware of our contract, and it is being upheld."

Mr. Cole pointed right at me.

Rude.

"The contract states no one under fifty will be allowed to take part in any of the events or mingle with your guests," Grant repeated robotically. "Emma is waiting in the foyer until after the raffle to give her mother a ride home. I felt it was unnecessary for her to wait in her car."

"And she isn't bothering any of the guests?"

"No, sir."

"She is standing right here," I muttered under my breath, and Mr. Cole's dark eyes shifted to me. A chill rushed down my spine.

Grant took a step slightly in front of me, drawing Mr. Cole's attention. "I assure you, she isn't bothering anyone."

"Fine." Mr. Cole grumbled and pulled his gaze away. "It would be a shame if I had to take my business elsewhere." He sneered in a way that was clearly a threat. "Now, what about the movie reels I asked for?"

"I haven't had any luck." Grant clenched a fist at his side. "I can find digital color remakes of several Cary Grant films but not the old film reels."

"No." He growled. "No digital remastered ones. It has to be authentic. Understood?"

Grant nodded. "I understand. I will keep looking."

Darian Cole offered me one last chilling glare before he stalked off.

I peeked around Grant to make sure Cole was out of earshot. "It's a shocker that man is single with such a charming personality."

Grant sighed as he plopped back down in his chair. "I hate working with him." His fists clenched, and his jaw was tight.

Looks like I needed to change the subject. "What movie reels did you need?"

"What?" Grant shook his head, resurfacing from his anger.

"Something about Cary Grant movie reels?"

"Oh yeah." He nodded the direction Mr. Cole had gone. "He wants authentic movie reels for an event. It can't be digital." He rubbed a hand down his face. "Where the crap am I supposed to find that?"

"I might have some at The Bees Knees. Do you know what ones you are looking for?"

He tipped his chin toward me. "Where is that? I might have checked there?"

My eyebrows lowered. "Maybe. It's a vintage thrift store downtown that I work at." My smile faltered. Wait! Was that where I had seen him before? "Were you in a few weeks ago?"

He chuckled. "Yeah, I think so. Just checked real quick and left, I think."

Thats why I kept thinking he felt familiar. "We get new inventory all the time, so I'm happy to check if you want." My phone vibrated. I pulled it out of my purse and smiled at my text. "It looks like Mom won the Latin dance class."

Grant's forehead creased. "Wait. I thought your mom's phone wasn't charged?" He didn't say a word.

"Maybe she charged it?" I forced a weak smile.

He waited with a raised brow.

"Or...maybe you were part of her payback for me setting her up?" I wrinkled my nose and squinted.

He tipped his chin and grinned. "I guess the apple doesn't fall far from the tree. A very dangerous and determined tree."

Chapter Eight

THE NEXT MORNING I CHANNELED MY INNER ROSIE THE Riveter in my high waisted jeans, polka dot button-up, and hair in a bandana.

I flipped through the tin film canisters at The Bees Knees, wondering if Grant would stop in today. *West Side Story*, *Casablanca*, *The Wizard of Oz*, and *Planet of the Apes*. Zero Cary Grant. My lips frowned. It was a long shot. Finding film reels from the 1940s and 1950s was hard, especially if you wanted them in playable condition.

I closed the drawer of film reels and stood. Maybe I could call some auction houses and see if they had anything coming up. Just in case.

Luckily, Mom forgave me after last night. I think winning dance lessons and a four-day cruise to Mexico next summer significantly helped the cause.

Humming along with the Johnny Cash record crooning through the store, I danced my way to the front and the Rolodex of business cards I kept under the cash register. I loved talking to Grant last night. He was this weird juxtaposition of soft and jagged edges.

The door chimed mid spin, and I froze.

Please don't be Grant.

I slowly finished the turn toward the door and was met with Jane's smile and raised brows. "Well, aren't you chipper today?" She lifted the two white coffee cups to indicate she brought breakfast. She followed me to the counter. "So, what happened?"

"What do you mean?" I flicked through the business cards, avoiding eye contact. If Jane found out I was acting this way due to a man, she would go nuts.

She tipped her chin and scrunched her brows. "The Kismet thing? Did you cancel and tell your mom like I told you to?" She set my cup on the counter and pushed it toward me.

I grabbed a few cards to make calls with later and set them by the cash register. "I didn't cancel. I know I should've, but I didn't." I picked up my cup and blew on the top. "I told Mom in the parking lot before going in, though, and that the tickets and information were correct." I shrugged. "Not great, but something..." I took a sip of my latte with soft top and caramel. It was still too hot.

"Well, at least that's something?" She nodded toward my drink. "Your coffee was practically white."

"Just how I like it." I blew into the steam.

She shook her head. "So what did your mom say?"

"Oh, she was livid." I grimaced. "And rightfully so."

Jane pointed at me with her coffee cup. "The way you run headstrong into everyone's dating life instead of focusing on your own has to be a sign of daddy issues or something." She took a sip.

"Daddy issues, not believing I'm lovable, abandonment. Pick a diagnosis and stick with it." I playfully stuck out my tongue.

"Maybe you have the trifecta." She grinned, taking a sip.

"Lucky me." I shrugged. "She said to focus on my own love life, and the next time I get asked on a date, I have to say yes and give it an 'honest try.'" I emphasized the last two words.

Jane raised a brow. "So, all I have to do is get someone to ask and you have to say yes?"

I grimaced. "I mean, technically, yes." I set the cup on the counter so I wasn't tempted to take another sip and burn my mouth.

Jane leaned against the front of the counter. "Hm, interesting. Did your mom go inside?"

"Yep. She said it was to waste the money I spent on tickets, and I had to come too." I chuckled.

"Wait. You went in too? So that means..." She set down her drink and slapped the counter. "Was that why you were spinning?" She drum-rolled her hands on the counter. "Mr. Muscles! You saw him again, didn't you? Oh. My. Gosh! Did he catch you? Did he throw you out? Was he as hot as you remember?" Jane rushed through the questions before running out of breath.

I grabbed my drink. I decided a burnt mouth was better than answering her questions. Hot, still too hot.

She squealed. "Oh my gosh! I'm right! You saw him!"

I raised my brow and blew on the cup.

"Drink later, talk now!" She reached across the counter and grabbed the drink from my hand, holding it hostage.

I sighed. "Fine. I told Mom I wasn't allowed to come, and she told me it never stopped me before."

"True." She gave me a cheeky grin.

I nodded. "So, after Mom met up with some guy named Robert, which I'm still not allowed to ask questions about, but I kid you not, there was a lot of blushing and hand brushing."

Jane's eyes widened and gestured for me to keep going.

"Well, I saw Grant...that's his name, Grant."

"Ooh la la." She raised her eyebrows and did a shoulder shimmy. "First name basis." She gasped. "Wait... Grant, as in Cary Grant!" She set my cup down and ran around the counter, grabbing my hands. "I need more details! Wait, I thought he was a jerk last time? Was he a jerk?"

"He wasn't last night." I paused, enjoying the annoyance grow in Jane's eyes as she waited.

"Ugh!" She threw her head back. "What does that mean? Come on...you're killing me!" Wait until I told her it was the same guy that she tried to get me to ask out.

I giggled. "Do you want me to talk?"

She furrowed her brows. "Of course I do, but you are taking your sweet time at doing it."

A ding at the front door sounded, and I turned to face the front counter.

"Oh, no you don't." Jane spun me back around to face her and didn't let go of my shoulders. "They will want to browse, anyway. You talk."

I rolled my eyes. "Mom made Grant babysit me last night."

"What?" She tipped her head to the side.

"Well, he wanted to kick me out. I asked Mom if she was ready to leave and she said no, pretended her phone was dead, and said that she needed me to wait for her." I rolled my eyes.

"Oh please, I'm sure you deserve all the meddling your mother wants to give you right now." Jane tipped her chin. "But what does that have to do with Muscles, or I guess Grant, babysitting you?"

"He had to stay with me and make sure I wasn't harassing any of the old guys. Do you know he actually believed I was there to find a date for me?" I shuddered.

Jane snorted. "Okay, so he is forced to hang out with you. Then what?" She put her hands to her mouth, trying to stop herself from interrupting again.

"I don't know. He felt different last night. We sat in the foyer for about thirty minutes and just talked. He was patient and kind. Not grumpy at all..."

Jane shook her head. "Guys are capable of that, you know." She pinched her lips and started clapping. "So, do you think you will see him again? Did you get his number?"

I raised my shoulders. "No number. I did tell him where I worked when he mentioned he was looking for film reels."

She wiggled her eyebrows. "Oh, so did he still look like a Greek god?"

"He did not disappoint." I gave a chef's kiss to my fingers.

Jane squealed. "Oh my gosh, ahhh! What if he comes here today? Will you ask for his number then?" She attempted to keep her excitement bottled up, which caused her to take quick little steps in place.

"I don't know. I couldn't stop smiling all night." He seemed sweet, but I don't think I was ready to risk my heart again. Then again, if he asked me out, I wouldn't be able to say no now.

A low clearing of a throat sound came from the front counter.

"Those are great questions." A deep familiar voice said from behind me.

My eyes widened.

Oh my gosh, please no...

I looked at Jane's opened mouth and wide eyes.

It was Grant—it had to be.

"Although I think I can answer the question of if I'm coming today," I heard Grant chuckle.

I turned slowly and saw Grant's smile, eyes full of mischief.

I whipped my head back around to Jane. "Why didn't you tell me he was there?" I whisper-yelled.

She shrugged. "I didn't see him. If you would have just hurried and told me the story, this wouldn't have happened." She peeked over my shoulder. "I see what you mean by the Greek god thing. Wait..." She peeked over my shoulder. "Is that the same guy from before? The one I said you should ask out." She whispered, not quit enough.

"Jane!"

This was not happening.

I steeled my shoulders and took a deep breath before I turned around, looking anywhere but Grant's face. "Oh hey, Grant." My voice was too high. I cleared my throat and fanned my heated face. "I, um, I didn't know you were here."

"Sorry, I didn't want to interrupt your conversation." I glanced at his face. He didn't look sorry with that grin.

"Oh I bet." I wiped my clammy hands on my jeans. He looked different today, and I was happy to report he looked just as yummy in jeans, black jacket over his arm, and a fitted t-shirt. The button ups were nice, but this way was easier to check out his arms.

Yep, he totally worked out.

Jane banged something against the desk behind me.

Oh geez! I was totally staring at his arms! Maybe he hadn't noticed? I glanced up to him, with his dark eyes and happy grin.

Yep. He definitely saw me checking out his arms.

Nailed it. I took a steadying breath. Focus!

"Um, I looked through the film reels this morning, and I don't have any Cary Grant tins." I glanced around the store and suddenly didn't know where to put my hands.

Grant nodded.

"Do you see anything else you like though?"

Grant's gaze fixed on me and he smiled. "Maybe." His low voice sent shivers down my spine.

Jane snorted behind me.

"No, that's not what I meant." I felt my skin heat, let out a tight breath, and gestured around the store. "I mean in the store."

He grinned. "Maybe I can look through the film reels you do have?"

"Right. Yep. I'll show you. It's over here." I turned to walk around the counter and met Jane's eyes. "Oh my gosh!" I mouthed with horror on my features. Then to Grant, "They are right over here." I walked to the front of the store that held the media section. I opened the drawer for Grant to look through. "I can call around to some auctions if you want. Did you know Cary Grant's real name is Archibald Leach?"

I was definitely rambling. I pursed my mouth to close.

He grinned. "I guess I should be grateful my parents didn't choose Archibald over Grant."

I snorted. "True."

His eyes scanned around the vintage store. "This place is pretty cool. I didn't really look around last time."

"Thanks. It's not mine. Not yet anyway." I shrugged. "I've worked here the last four years, and I love it."

He stopped studying his surroundings and started studying me.

"Before I make a fool of myself, you're not dating anyone, right?" Grant fidgeted with the arm sleeve of his jacket.

I glanced up and was happy to see him look nervous. He always seemed so collected. "Well..." I drew the word out, and Grant looked at the ceiling. "I thought about Mr. Hanen, but I'm not sure I can get over the feet thing." I tapped a finger to my chin in thought.

Grant shook his head, chuckled, and took a step closer to me.

Please say I don't have coffee breath.

"In that case, do you want to go to dinner tonight?"

This suddenly felt less playful, "Um, well..."

He looked at me, and I couldn't look away. He didn't push, just waited for my answer.

Of all the guys that could have asked me next. Why him?

Grant was gorgeous and seemed kind and caring. It would be all the worse when he decided he didn't like me.

"Yes!" Jane called from the counter of the store.

I glared in her direction.

"Remember your mom..." she called sweetly.

Why had I told her that?

I took a tight breath. "Um, sure. Dinner sounds great." I held the breath in my chest. "I'm off at six if tonight works."

Holy crap! I guess this was happening. So much for the no dating rule. If I had to break it though...Grant seemed a worthy choice. It could be fun while it lasted.

"Six." Grant smiled, and reached out and grabbed my hand in

his, giving it a light squeeze. "I will be back at six then." He winked as he threw on his jacket.

I tried to contain my smile, but my body didn't get the memo. "Sounds great."

He smiled, nodded at me, and walked past me to the exit.

Jane cheered in the background before the door finished swinging closed.

What would it feel like to have a man like Grant hold me?

"This might be a very bad idea."

How long would it be until I had to choose between him or being me?

Chapter Nine

I LOOKED IN THE BATHROOM MIRROR AT THE BEES Knees and applied another layer of lip gloss. I really needed Rosie the Riveter energy tonight; hopefully she would help me be brave with that "can do" attitude and not make a fool of myself.

5:45 p.m.

I exhaled slowly.

My phone vibrated. Was it Grant canceling? My stomach did flips and unleashed butterflies, letting me know I wasn't sure what I wanted. I grabbed my phone out of my back pocket.

It was Mom.

I answered. "Hey, Mom."

"I talked to Jane." I could hear Spike meowing in the background.

"Of course you did." I put her on speaker and set the phone on the counter.

"Remember, you promised to try."

I could imagine Mom and her stern finger waving at me as I stared in the mirror and pinched a curl, using my mouth to open a bobby pin. "I'm going—what else do you want from me?"

"For starters, stop pretending you want to live in the fifties."

I grabbed the ends of the handkerchief headband and tightened it. "What do you mean?"

"In the fifties women couldn't hold most jobs, couldn't serve as jurors, couldn't own property, and there wasn't even birth control. You don't want to go back in time as a woman."

I thought of my prized independence that I enjoyed. "You're right, I don't actually want the fifties." I picked up the phone. "I want someone who acts like a gentleman." I left the bathroom and went to close the till for the day. "Someone to open the door for me, give me a jacket when I'm cold, and to accept me for me." I turned the small key on the old till with the faded yellow buttons, opening the cash drawer.

Mom sighed. "You can and should expect those things, but the men of the romantic movies in the fifties, and today for that matter, aren't real." I could hear dishes clanging in the background. "Real men are far more complicated, frustrating, and wonderful. They are real, and that's what you want. Trust me, you want something real. And in real life it takes time to get to know a person."

I huffed as I grabbed the money out of the drawer. "I do want something that's real, but I want something that lasts. I want to be able to feel good in my skin when I'm with them. I want to feel like they appreciate me partly because of my idiosyncrasies, not in spite of them. I want to feel like he wants to be with all of me... Maybe that's still too big of an ask, though." I put the bills into the envelope and grabbed my phone off the counter.

"The more time I give it, the more potential it has to hurt when they don't choose me." I rubbed my forehead. I didn't want to put myself through this again. What if after that time, I had to fight to stay true to myself?

"Not when, Em. If."

I felt the tension build behind my chest. I put the money into the safe.

Could it be if and not when?

I walked to the back of the store and grabbed my jacket and purse, turning off the lights.

"You are uniquely beautiful. You love being independent, and you love vintage furniture, black and white movies, and so much more. You are not cookie-cutter, and neither is your date. It takes time. Be yourself and learn who he is. Then if it doesn't work, you will know it's because you weren't compatible. But you won't ever know if you don't try."

I took a deep breath. Mom was right, like always. "Love you, Mom." I flipped the OPEN sign to CLOSED. "I promise I'll try." My hands were already jittery with nerves.

"That's all I ask. Love you, Emma."

"So does this mean we're even, then?" I gave a nervous laugh.

Mom scoffed. "That depends on how it goes tonight."

Message received. I'm not let off the hook until I give this an honest try.

I locked the front door and double checked it was secure. "All right, I need to go, Mom."

"Okay, bye honey, have fun."

I dropped my phone into my purse and saw Grant walking down the sidewalk toward me.

My throat went dry at the sight of him. Cary Grant had high cheekbones, stiff side-parted hair, and tailored suits. This Grant was the opposite in a lot of ways with his black sports jacket, tapered jeans, and loose, wavy, and soft brown hair. And he was beautiful.

All right, Rosie, don't fail me now.

He stepped up beside me and held out his arm for me. "Do you like Italian?"

My mouth instantly watered, and not only from Grant's good looks, or how he was looking at me. "Love it." I slid my arm through his elbow and walked beside him. Being this close, I noticed my head was even with his shoulder. He smelled like soap and leather.

"Perfect." He led me down the street. "Let's go to my favorite place, then."

He looked down at me and smiled.

"Sounds great." I smiled back, and my glossy lips didn't even quiver.

"You are beautiful."

Holy Cannoli! This man was setting me on fire.

I pinched my lips. "You're not too bad yourself."

We continued down the sidewalk. "So, what's your favorite movie?" Grant asked.

I cringed. Ugh! Why did he start there? I would rather start with color. My answer would be normal. "I'm sure it's not your style."

He tilted his head toward me. "Try me."

"Well, ones with Cary Grant, for starters." I felt heat warm my cheeks. "I like *Roman Holiday, Gone with the Wind, To Catch a Thief, Fiddler on the Roof...*" I paused, waiting for him to stop me. "I also like *Emma* or any Jane Austen or Charles Dickens adaptation. Oh, and musicals!" Grant's lips pulled down and I chuckled. "It's fine. I know, I have unusual movie tastes." It was fine.

"I technically saw some *Fiddler on the Roof.*" He grimaced. "My mom tricked me into watching part of it when I was younger. I'm sorry, but it was so boring."

I chuckled. "You were probably too young to understand its brilliance." I bumped his shoulder. "How about you? What movies do you like?"

He pressed the crossing button, and we waited at the street corner. "I like action movies like Jason Bourne, Marvel, oh, and the Transformers movies were good. Not as good as the old cartoon, though."

I hadn't seen any of those either. Oh, wait. "I saw *Thor* with an old boyfriend. It was pretty funny."

What?! I stutter stepped as we began across the street. Why had I brought up old boyfriends? My face burned, and I refused to meet Grant's eyes. We walked past a group of teenagers racing on scooters.

Curiosity got the better of me, and I peeked up at him. He wasn't going to take the bait. I rose to the challenge. "What about you? Have you seen a black and white movie with a girlfriend, maybe?" I forced my face into confidence I didn't feel.

Grant smirked. "Not yet." He winked.

A rush of tingles ran up my spine. He reached for the door handle beside us and held it open, allowing me to go through first.

I was wrapped in the aroma of a garlic bread hug. "It smells delicious!" I looked at the sign above the hostess. Leo's Pasta. "I love Leo's!" I had never actually been inside the restaurant though.

"Same." Grant added. "Have you tried their bread dipped in balsamic vinegar?"

"Nope." I shook my head.

"It's so good. You have to try it." Grant turned to the hostess. "Two, please."

She looked down at her chart, nodded, and grabbed two menus. "Follow me please."

We followed her through the room with dark wood accents, grapevine painted wallpaper, and low-lit booths to our table.

I sat and took the menu she handed me. No need to prove I had the one on my fridge memorized.

Looking over Grant's shoulder, I noticed Peter, the man who delivered my takeout. His kind eyes and happy smile lit up with recognition.

Crap! Grant was soon going to know just how much I loved Leo's.

I ducked my head, hoping that Peter hadn't recognized me.

"Emma!" He came to my side.

Guess I wasn't so lucky. I peeked up at him and smiled.

"It's good you came to see me this time." He chuckled.

I met Grant's curious gaze over the table. My cheeks burned with embarrassment. "I told you I liked it here. Hey, Peter."

Grant chuckled.

"Hey! No movie date night tonight, eh?" Peter raised his eyebrows and gestured toward Grant.

I put both hands over my face, wishing I could melt into the floor.

"Nice to meet you. I'm Grant." Grant held out his hand toward Peter.

I peeked up to see Peter's mouth drop open with excitement as he shook his hand. "Grant?" Peter pointed excitedly at me. "His name is Grant. Guys," Peter hollered back to the kitchen. "Emma has found herself a Grant." Whoops and cheers came from the back and I hid my face behind my hands.

Well, this was definitely me being me. I guess we were going to test the leaving theory right out the gate.

"No, Peter. He isn't my Grant, just Grant." I held my hands up. Grant smirked. He was obviously enjoying the exchange.

Peter waved me off. "Not yet, eh?" He nudged Grant's shoulder.

"Exactly." Grant grinned.

What did he mean by that?

It was past time to change the subject. "I think I need some water, Peter." I was way too sweaty to be socially acceptable. I fanned my face.

Grant pinched his lips in a failed attempt to hide a smile.

"You bet! And what for you, Grant?" Peter smirked.

"Water is great, thank you."

Peter practically skipped away.

"So you have a lot of guys over for date nights with Leo's Pasta at your place?" Grant's eyebrows raised.

"Nope." I grimaced. "It's much more pathetic..."

His eyebrows scrunched together.

I ran my fingers through my hair. "I order Leo's takeout and watch Cary Grant movies in my apartment by myself. It's kinda my weekend routine. I joke with Peter that it's my Cary Grant date night." I scrunched my nose. If Grant ditched me now, I would make Peter give me a ride home.

"Why is that worse?" He tipped his head to the side.

"Seems dramatic and lonely when I say it out loud." I smiled. "I think it sounds better if I had dates over for them."

"That probably depends on who you ask." Grant gave me a wicked grin. "I've never seen a Cary Grant movie. I didn't even know he existed before this whole Kismet thing."

I did my best to pretend I wasn't dying of embarrassment. "Well, you may get lucky at my place and get to watch one."

"Hey, I'm game." He wiggled his eyebrows up and down.

Wait... What?

"You're game for what?" Surely he wasn't talking about watching a black-and-white movie tonight.

He smiled showing off his dimple. "Getting lucky at your place or watching a movie. Both sound like a win-win..."

Wait. Oh. My. Gosh.

Did I really say that!

"Wait, What? That is not what I meant!" I could feel the heat burning my cheeks and I covered my face with my hands.

"Um..." I huffed out a slow breath.

He chuckled. "Unless you didn't mean to invite me over to your apartment to watch a movie, when you don't know me..."

I blanched.

"Uh, yeah..."

He chuckled and winked. "Maybe next time." He dropped the subject.

My posture relaxed as I let out a breath I had been holding.

Peter returned with our drinks and we ordered.

"So, your turn to talk awkwardly about your ex?" I grimaced.

"I've been dating mainly casually the last few years." He shrugged. "I've had serious relationships before, but I'm also assuming I have a few years on you." He raised a brow, asking my age.

"I'm twenty-two."

He nodded. "Twenty-nine."

Peter brought out bread and Grant asked for extra balsamic in the oil. He ripped off a piece of bread and used it to stir the mixture and then scraped it against the side of the dish and placed it in his mouth.

"So good." He looked to the ceiling and slid some bread over to me. "Try it."

I followed his lead. It was an interesting mixture of bitter and sweet. "Not bad, but I think it's hard to beat warm bread and soft butter." I shrugged. "So, what changed the dating routine in the last few years?" I spread some butter on my bread, as he dipped another piece in the vinegar and oil.

He finished his bite. "My dad died."

I tipped my chin trying to connect the invisible dots. "And you needed to help your mom?"

He scoffed. "No, for the first time, I didn't have to help my mom."

I picked up another piece of bread and spread butter on it. "I'm not following."

"Long story short, my dad was a jerk. I'm happy he is gone." His lowered eyes flicked to mine. "This is probably not the best first date material."

"Is it any better than inviting a stranger to your apartment?" I shook my head and rolled my eyes.

Grant raised his left shoulder. "Well, with my portion of Dad's life insurance money and what I had saved, I bought the venue, The Brick House, and restored it."

I thought about what that would cost. "So you've been too busy starting a business to date?" He nodded. "The few times I've been there it seems like you've done a wonderful job. I love the mix of warm wood tones, bricks, and industrial." I licked the crumbs off my fingers.

"The few times you were there sneaking around and diving

under tables, you mean." He shook his head. "But thank you. It has had a lot of unforeseen challenges, but I'm still glad I took it on." He traced the wood grain of the table with his right pointer finger. "And I'm pretty sure only part of it is because I want to prove my dad wrong." He exhaled slowly and grabbed the back of his neck with his left hand. "Enough of that, now. What's your favorite color?"

"Blue."

Peter soon brought out our food, and I had him cover my cheese ravioli with parmesan.

"So tell me about The Bees Knees and your obsession with the old movies." He smiled and reached his other hand out across the table, holding his palm up and fingers open, waiting to let me place my hand in his.

I stared at his hand—should I take it? I looked up to his face and was met with his kind eyes, a smile, and that blasted dimple.

Oh what the heck, why not? I put my hand in his.

Chapter Ten

I ROLLED OVER IN MY SOFT PINK COMFORTER AND reached blindly for my phone. I had missed calls from Jane and Mom and several texts. Jane had called at 10 p.m., technically last night—but at the time I was still somehow with Grant.

I clicked on Jane's messages from today.

Jane: Em, if you're dead right now, I'm going to be so mad.

Jane: That's it, I'm coming over and if you are not home, I'm calling the police.

Whoa. I sat up in bed and rubbed the sleep from my eyes.

Emma: Sorry I didn't call back last night, and I was sleeping this morning. You know it's like 5:30 a.m., right?

Three dots blinked as Jane wrote her reply.

Jane: Oh my gosh, I was going to call the police. You can't do that to me.

I crisscrossed my legs and smiled as I thought through the night before. It felt a bit like a dream. Everything seemed brighter.

Emma: Yeah, sorry. When you called last night, we were still hanging out, and by the time I got home I fell right into bed.

Jane: oh...

Jane: OH!!!!

Jane: So it was good then, yes?!

I giggled. After Leo's we spent well over an hour walking around downtown. We talked about everything and nothing at the same time.

Emma: Yeah, it was good.

Jane: I NEED MORE DETAILS

I plopped back on my pillows and looked at the ceiling, not able to contain my smile.

Emma: Well he asked if I had plans tomorrow afternoon? I think we are going to check out a few vintage shops to look for the film reels he needs.

Jane: AHHHHHHHHHH!

Jane: Okay, was he nice? I mean other than looking, because we know that. She sent a flame emoji.

I bit my bottom lip and thought of him holding doors open for me, how he insisted he walk on the traffic side of sidewalks, and that he escorted me to my car.

Emma: It was perfect. He was a perfect gentleman.

Jane sent a string of emojis, from party streamers to dancing to kisses.

I needed to get ready for work, and all this would be better in person. I got out of bed and went to start the shower.

Emma: I need to shower but maybe you can come by the shop on your lunch break?

Jane: I will be there!! So happy for you, Em!

I was happy too. It was fun playing Cupid, but I never got this rush of nerves and butterflies. What if it all ends as fast as it started?

Emma: But what happens if it's all in my head? What if he doesn't feel the same? What if he likes me at the start but he changes his mind?

I tried to remind myself to let it play out. I rubbed my hand through my hair and bounced my leg. I was quickly spiraling, and I knew it. And Jane knew it.

Jane: Em, deep breaths. All those things are the future's job to figure out. You don't get to know the ending from the start. No one does. Right now your job is to shower, lean in to hope, and be excited!!!! Cya at lunch!

I was thankful for the millionth time that Jane was in my life. I took a deep breath and hopped in the shower.

The day dragged on at work and flew by too quickly at the same time. At lunch Jane and I picked apart every possible interaction for double meaning. I couldn't wait to see Grant tomorrow, but I was also terrified.

I wiped down the shelves of assorted china. My phone vibrated in my pocket, and I saw a text from Grant. The butterflies in my stomach and the quickened beat of my heart confirmed it—I was definitely feeling something for him.

Grant: Excited to see you tomorrow. Do you want me to pick you up or meet you at Boise Pawn and Thrift?

Emma: Do you have a preference?

Grant: I'm happy with whatever makes you feel most comfortable.

I glanced to the side and chewed on my bottom lip. Riding together meant more time spent together. And after talking to Jane and Mom, I promised them both I would try to give it time to see if it could work.

Emma: I'm fine to ride with you, but parking can be nasty near my apartment.

Grant: I'm sure I'll manage.

He wasn't a man of many words. I chuckled.

Emma: Deal.

Grant: Is it okay if we start around noon? I have a few things in the morning first.

Emma: Yep, noon is great!

I sent him my address and got back to dusting.

The store had never been cleaner.

I SHOOK OUT MY HANDS TO CALM MY NERVES. WHY WAS I so nervous to see Grant? I put in my pearl stud earrings and added a coat of my pink lip gloss. I tucked my light blue shirt into my high-waisted jeans and tied a light pink scarf in my hair. Our date was only two days ago, and we'd texted in between, so why did this feel different?

Deep breaths.

I didn't get to know the ending early.

I repeated the phrases Jane gave me.

A knock sounded from my front door, and I took a calming breath.

"Coming," I hollered toward the door as I grabbed my cardigan and purse from off the hooks.

I opened the door and felt the cool spring air swirl around me. Grant was giving me serious James Dean vibes with his leather jacket and jeans. So yummy.

"You ready?" His eyes drank me in, and I felt beautiful without him saying a word.

"Yep." I nodded and locked the door behind me. He held his hand out for me again, palm up, waiting. It was a bold gesture, but respectful, and I loved it.

I set my hand in his and grinned as his hand enveloped mine, soft but firm, and when his thumb started tracing mine I lost all coherent thought and my steps stuttered again.

"Whoops," I chuckled, "guess I'd better pay attention."

He winked and led me down the rest of the stairs to his black Chevy truck. "I like that color on your lips." His eyes were on my mouth, and I tried to swallow.

"Oh, um. Thanks." My heart was trying to sprint out of my chest.

He opened the truck door for me and waited for me to sit,

then he shut the door and went around the front of the vehicle. The car smelled like him, a mix of leather and something earthy. I took a quick peek around. For a single guy, his car was pretty clean. There was a gym bag in the back and a trash bag that looked to be full of Red Bulls. Grant opened his door, drawing my attention back to him.

He smiled and shifted his truck into drive and merged onto State Street. We drove the twenty minutes to the thrift store, relaying stories from elementary school. He pulled into the parking lot.

"This is kind of a long shot to find film canisters, but I figure it's worth a try." I shrugged.

"Sounds good." He stepped out of his truck.

I had called three auction houses and asked them to watch for movie reels, but so far no luck.

Grant made his way around to me.

Should I wait for him to open my door? Was that weird? Should I just open it?

He was coming my way, but the stress of sitting there waiting got the better of me, and I opened the door. Grant took the last three steps between us and held out his hand for me.

"So, is this what you call casual dating?" I lifted our joined hands.

He smirked. "Nope." He led us to the glass door of the thrift store and opened it. I pinched my lips tight to keep from squealing and forced my breaths to slow. Holy hotcakes!

The treasure hunt began. Guitars, jewelry, records, bikes, and questionable clothing. Each new corner held limitless possibilities.

Grant found a Metallica poster he liked, but no film reels. The day continued in the same scavenger hunt fashion as we went to three other thrift stores.

No film reels older than the eighties.

"Worth the try?" I asked Grant as we made our way back to the truck.

"I don't regret how I've spent my day, if that's what you're asking." He grinned down at me, and I wanted to reach up and run my fingers through his trimmed facial hair along his jawline.

Wow...um, weird. I cleared my throat. "So, did you get your errands done this morning?"

"Some of them." He held the door open for me, and I slid into his truck. He came around, sat in his seat, and shifted the truck into drive.

"I have a few things I still need to do at The Brick House later." He held his hand out for me and I took it. "But I got my workout in." He smiled proudly. "You hungry?"

It was 4 p.m. "I could snack." I shrugged. "The Brick House is between here and my apartment. We could stop there on the way if you'd like?"

He shook his head no. "In some ways that would be great, but I'm trying to enforce some boundaries with work and my personal life. I think bringing you to work with me is cheating." He side-eyed me.

"Even if I was the one who offered?" I reached out and touched his arm. "I would love nothing better than to snoop around the place without the fear of being thrown out."

He steeled his shoulders. "Okay, it should only take me thirty minutes, but once I walk in those doors, it's like everything falls apart and takes longer than I think it will." He grimaced. "Maybe I should just go back later tonight."

"Hmm..." I pinched my lips. "We could set a timer? I've heard it works wonders for toddlers."

"Funny." He rolled his eyes.

"Really, I would like to see it again, so I don't mind."

"Okay, just don't let me talk to anyone about the water lines..." His shoulders stiffened. "And we are setting a timer."

"Deal." I clapped.

After grabbing some sodas and fries, we got to The Brick House around 5 p.m.

It was such a beautiful building. "Why did you buy this building specifically?" I asked as he reached for my hand and led me through the parking lot.

"Timing and history." We went up the steps. "They were going to tear it down. I wanted to save it. That, and I got a really good deal on it. But," he said as he held the door for me, "turns out it was more broken than I thought."

As we stepped inside the glass doors, he grabbed his phone out of his pocket and started a thirty-minute timer, tipping his phone to show me. "Okay, only thirty minutes. I'm not joking, this place is a time-sucker."

I followed him to his office and sat in a soft chair as he paid a bill, grabbed some paperwork, and sent a few emails. The timer went off, but then I convinced him to give me a tour. A team of decorators was walking around the different ballrooms, setting up for the next Kismet event. I watched as a group of people in blue polos carried boxes of disco balls and fog machines.

"So how did you end up doing the Kismet events?" I squeezed Grant's hand in mine. Somehow, even though it was so new, his hand was starting to feel familiar.

"It was that or bankruptcy." He shrugged. "We had a bunch of flooding behind some walls after opening, water damage everywhere, last-minute cancellations of events, refunds, and insurance considered it pre-existing damages." We walked down the main stairs to the foyer. "Cash flow was nonexistent, and then word spread that the venue was having problems and we stopped getting calls for events."

"Ouch."

He rubbed his hand through his hair and looked down at me. "I asked Darian Cole as a last-ditch effort to save the place." His jaw tightened. "He said yes as a favor to my dad, after I gave it to him at barely above cost." He shook his head. "I hate working with him—he reminds me so much of Dad. But he's all I got right now. And if this place fails..."

I reached up and ran my hand down his clenched arm. "What does it mean if it fails?" It felt far more than just financial.

His stance was rigid and his eyes were hard. "This is my last chance to prove my dad wrong."

I leaned my head against his shoulder. Thinking of what to say, I took a slow breath. "Grant. Your dad's dead. I'm pretty sure he has zero opinions on your business venture." I looked up to his tired eyes and hoped he could let out some of the anger and pain. "And even if he does, it sounds like he was a miserable man. You shouldn't care what he thinks."

"True." The topic sagged his shoulders. "I know logically that I need to let him and my anger go, but it keeps seeping in."

"Tell me about your mom."

His shoulders eased. "She is great, honestly. I should go see her more than I do. That's the other thing I'm trying to do better at." He grinned, as I followed him to the truck. "Where to, or are you sick of me yet?" Grant bumped against my shoulder.

It was 6 p.m. We had been together for six hours, and I'd hardly felt the time pass. "Are you up for a Grant movie date night?"

His eyes met mine. "Time to meet the competition, eh?"

I chuckled. "If you can handle it. The men from that era set a pretty high bar..." I remembered what Mom said about the difference between real and fiction. "You know, except the whole women couldn't own property or attend college." I grimaced.

Grant smirked. "Yeah, they sound like real charmers." His fingers curled gently around mine as he lifted my hand to his lips. He hesitated, I could feel the warmth of his breath against my skin. My breath hitched, and he pressed a slow, soft kiss to my skin. Warmth radiated from his lips, up my arm, and into my chest, making it impossible to look away.

Holy Casanova, this man!

Chapter Eleven

Back at my apartment, we put in an order to Leo's Pasta. I thought about branching out, but Grant insisted on the authentic Cary Grant movie date night experience.

He sat on a pink swivel stool and looked around my apartment with a contented smile. "It feels very you."

It was me. From the vintage movie posters to the mint mixer.

"So why were you setting up your mom?" Grant eyed me curiously.

"Last string of guys I dated, things started good, but soon they began belittling my interests, size, or they cheated, so..." I pursed my lips. "I decided playing Cupid was far more fun and safe, but I ran out of single friends." I shrugged. "Between that and the vision of my mom happy and spoiled..."

Grant spun the chair around so he was facing me. "What made you change your mind?"

I grinned. "Mom."

He waited for me to continue.

"After the whole Kismet thing, that was part of my forgiveness agreement. I had to say yes to the next person who asked me on a date, and I had to give it an 'honest try.'" I did air quotes around it.

"Would you have said no to a date with me without your mom's demands?"

"Yep." My lips pinched. "Dating feels easier to avoid than finding the right fit. Do you have a specific movie in mind?"

He stood, stepping toward me with a contemplative gaze. "How about whichever you saw first if you have it?" He reached out to me and I placed my hand in his.

"That would be *My Favorite Wife*." I nodded. "So why the change in dating for you?" I led him to the couch.

"Honestly, it was your mom for me as well."

I stopped and turned to face him. "My mom?

"Yeah." He stepped next to me and brushed his hand along my cheek. "Sounds crazy, but in that moment when she asked what I would do if she was my mom...it kinda shook the crazy possessed hold that work had on me." He nodded to the couch and we both sat, my legs brushing up against his. "I remembered I hadn't called my mom in weeks. I remembered part of my plan was to have a better balance with work and life."

There was a knock on the door, and I went and opened it. Peter was giddy when he saw Grant standing behind me. "I didn't think this was all for you." He held up the bags of food. I grabbed the bags and set them on the coffee table. "I even threw in some extra cupcakes." He leaned toward Grant. "She loves chocolate cupcakes."

Grant grinned. "I appreciate any help I can get." Grant chuckled and grabbed some cash from his pocket. He paid the bill and tip before I got the chance.

"I'm happy to pay—at the very least for my portion."

Grant shook his head. "This one is on me."

Peter smiled, winked in my direction, and whistled as he left.

I set dishes on the coffee table and laid out napkins. After eating and both of us cleaning up the dishes, we returned to the couch. I pressed play and grabbed a blanket from the corner and sat. Grant sat beside me and slid his arm across the back of the couch.

The classical music filled the room and a hand on the screen began changing cards with the actors' and actresses' names on them.

Grant shot me a puzzled look. "You can see the hand of the person changing the cards."

I chuckled. "Yeah, really high tech."

"Huh, weird."

My leg brushed against his, I moved my head onto his chest, and I felt his chest expand in a deep breath. Leaning against him, I could feel him chuckle at the witty lines of the movie. He was watching one of my movies, and he liked it. How was this real life?

I glanced up into his eyes, and Grant must have felt my gaze. His eyes met mine. His gaze dropped to my mouth, and I licked my lips.

One side of his mouth pulled up into a smile as he met my eyes again. "You're dangerous."

"How so..." I stared at Grant's mouth, my throat unable to swallow.

Mom was right. This was way better than playing Cupid, or fantasies about a pretend movie star. This was real, and I didn't want it to end. I bit into my bottom lip and stared up at him.

I sighed...loud enough that he heard me.

His eyes dropped down to mine and I gasped and covered my mouth with my hand. His dimple was showing in all its glory, begging me to kiss it. I closed my eyes to remove the temptation and counted to three. I desperately needed to get a hold of myself.

We finished *My Favorite Wife* and then I decided it was only fair for me to watch one of his shows. He picked *Iron Man* and we started the next movie.

"So, are these chocolate cupcakes really that good?" Grant asked.

I pulled off the wrapper, licking the chocolate frosting from my fingers. "They are terrible. You won't even like it." I smiled.

He rolled his eyes. "Maybe just let me have a bite of yours. I don't want a whole one."

"Okay, but if you change your mind, then I get a bite of yours." I made a serious face. I was not getting swindled out of my cupcake by some brown eyes and a gorgeous smile.

I held the unwrapped cupcake toward him. He leaned closer, and I felt the warmth of his breath on my hands. I watched as his mouth closed around a bite of the cupcake. My stomach dropped. He pulled away from the cupcake with a small smudge of chocolate on the left side of his mouth. His forehead creased and he rapidly shook his head.

"Nope."

"What are you talking about? How could you not love these?" I took a bite of the cupcake, and the silky frosting coated my tongue. "Seriously, so good."

Grant shivered. "Whoa, way too sweet." He shook his head. "It's all yours." His eyes went down to my mouth. "You got a little..." His thumb brushed across my bottom lip, burning and freezing at the same time. Then his eyes locked on to mine, and I watched him swallow. He didn't move his hand.

"You're no better." I shifted closer and brushed the chocolate from the corner of his mouth, and then I licked it off my thumb. After all, I wouldn't waste chocolate.

His eyes burned as he gazed at my mouth. "Emma." It came out between a growl and a whisper. "I've kept myself from kissing you several times today, but if you lick frosting off your fingers like that..." He closed his eyes and took a deep, steadying breath.

I raised a brow and grinned. "Like what? Like this?" I put a bit of frosting on the tip of my index finger before I slowly brought it to my mouth.

Grant stared at my lips. "I wouldn't." His lips parted as his eyes focused on my mouth.

"Wouldn't what?" I raised the finger to my lips. "This?" I batted my eyelashes as I licked off the frosting.

He made a guttural sound deep in his throat as he leaned toward me, and I had to remind myself to breathe. I didn't think anyone had looked at me quite like that. "I'm going to kiss you now, unless you tell me otherwise." With such a gentlemanly warning, I placed my cupcake down without breaking eye contact and he put his large hands on my waist and pulled me closer. I stared into his eyes, our faces so close that our noses brushed. He put his hand on the back of my neck and the other one brushed along my cheek. His eyes devoured mine. Then he paused, giving me a second to stop if I wanted to, but I definitely didn't.

I reached and ran my hand down his scratchy jaw line, savoring the rough texture. Grant leaned closer to my mouth. I was still too far away, I needed to reach his face better. I kneeled on the couch and ran one hand through his hair, the soft brown strands flowing through my fingers. I placed the other hand on the back of his neck. He was so close, I could feel each rapid inhale of his chest and I watched his eyes desperately studying mine. The smell of chocolate mingling with his scent of earth and leather wrapped itself tighter around me.

His lips inched closer and parted a breath away from mine.

Then he grabbed my hips, pulling me onto his lap. My lips fell into his and the warmth of his arms circled me. His chest was hard as it pressed against mine, trying to pull me even closer to him.

Grant nipped at my bottom lip, and I gasped before I returned the gesture. The tip of his tongue traced the edge of my bottom lip and I savored the taste of him.

The energy changed and his lips were on my neck trailing down to my collar bone leaving a burning trail in their wake. I couldn't get enough of him. I brought his mouth back to mine and the kiss softened. Our foreheads rested against each other. I stared into his brown eyes as he rubbed my back.

"Emma, you're so beautiful." It came out as a rough whisper.

I slid my hands over his jawline. He closed his eyes and leaned into my touch.

"There's a reason we call you Mr. Muscles." I traced a finger along his arm with a smile, feeling the strength beneath. "You know you're gorgeous, right? I still don't get why you're here with me." I leaned back, remembering how this would one day end. One day hurt.

His eyebrows dipped down and he eyes locked with mine. "What are you talking about?"

Ugh! I was totally ruining this moment.

"Grant, you are basically a Greek god. Any woman would melt in your arms." I looked down at myself sitting on his lap. "I'm not every man's cup of tea." I shrugged.

"First off, tea's gross. It's basically drinking watered-down grass." He brushed his fingers along my chin until I looked up at him. "Secondly, why?"

I huffed. "I don't know." I glanced at the ceiling. "Maybe because I'm eccentric, weird, and curvy? The guys I dated—they hated my movie taste, they started liking me, but then I think they wanted me to be more...normal?"

He ran his hands down the curves of my sides, and I fought the urge to suck in. "You're wrong." He growled against my throat. "I think you've spent too much time with insecure little boys." He kissed my throat.

I tipped my head to the side, giving him better access to the curve of my neck.

"You are beautiful. I love that you know who you are and what you like. It's sexy. And personally..." He raised his brows and gave me a wicked grin. "I really enjoy your curves."

I chuckled.

He held my face in his strong hands and looked into my eyes. "So, let's try again." He paused and looked me in the eyes. "Emma, you are beautiful."

I couldn't stop my smile and his hungry eyes shot to my lips again. "Thanks!" I giggled and pulled him to my mouth so I could kiss him. "You're not so bad yourself." I whispered into his ear.

"Mr. Muscles?" He shook his head. "Really?"

"Do you prefer Greek god?"

He rolled his eyes. "That's just ridiculous."

Several kisses later, I heard an explosion coming from the movie behind me. "I think you're right," I whispered into his ear.

"About what?" His nose was pressed against my throat, smelling my skin.

"This might be my new favorite movie." I nudged my nose against his.

Grant growled and nipped at my ear. "Okay, now you actually have to watch it."

I giggled as I slid off his lap, and he wrapped his arms around me as we refocused on watching the movie.

I tilted my head up and kissed him on his dimple. "Fine, I'll stop kissing you and actually watch."

His eyes dropped to my kiss-swollen lips. "Doubt it."

Chapter Twelve

Sunday morning Jane called, asking me to go shopping.

"You hate shopping."

She sighed and I could feel the heaviness in her voice. "Finn and I broke up. I just want a distraction."

"Uh, wait…" I thought things were going better. "I'm so sorry." Finn obviously was stupid. When people didn't choose the real me I could understand, but someone not wanting Jane—that was straight-up crazy.

I heard her voice catch through the phone. "He was so great at first, but he never made time to be with me. It was always one excuse or another. Half the time I felt like he pretended he didn't even know me. I figured if he wanted to be together he would put time in."

I sighed.

Wow.

"Jane, I am so sorry."

If Finn wasn't willing to sacrifice time to be with Jane, what was the chance that Grant would do the same in the long run? I shook my head. I needed to focus on Jane right now.

"I think they have the farmer's market starting up on the Grove?" I sat up in bed and ran a hand through my hair. "Give me thirty and I will be ready."

Jane agreed. "Maybe I will go for a run and just meet you at your house, then."

I was dying to tell Jane all about Grant and how he'd kissed me and said I was beautiful, but this wasn't the right time.

Jane would shop with me, but it wasn't what she really wanted to do. I sighed. "Do you want me to run with you?" I could barely hold back the terror in my voice.

There was a pause. "What?"

"Look, I don't want to run, but if you want me with you, I will gasp for air like a dying fish behind you as you tell me all the ways Finn is a jerk."

"You would run with me?" Jane cheered.

"Well, I will be running," I shook my head. "You would probably be walking. Just to give proper expectations."

Jane chuckled. "Aw, Em, what would I do without you?"

"For starters, run a lot faster." I added.

She laughed. "Grab your shoes! We're going running!"

Was it wrong to hope she pulled a muscle on her way to my house?

THREE DAYS LATER, AS I SHIFTED MY SWOLLEN AND bruised ankle on the coffee table, the bag of ice fell to the floor.

Drat! I rotated to grab the bag while keeping my ankle elevated.

"I got it." Grant leaned forward on the couch and picked up the bag of ice, setting it on top of my ankle.

"As if me being chased by a goose wasn't punishment enough."

I resituated on the couch, trying to ease the throbbing. "Those birds are scary. How long is this going to take?"

Grant fluffed the pillow behind me. "It happened only a few days ago. Give it a week and you will be good as new." He leaned forward and kissed the top of my forehead. "I wouldn't run on it for a bit longer, though."

"You say that like I plan on running ever again." I rolled my eyes as I readjusted the pillow at my side.

Grant raised his shoulder. "Whether you run is up to you. But take it easy in case you have a...what did you call it? Major mental relapse from kissing me." He chuckled as he brushed his thumb along my bottom lip and leaned down and pressed his lips softly to mine.

This still felt like a dream too good to be true, and I didn't want this dream to end.

"I don't plan to stop kissing you." His lips curved into a smile as he leaned forward and pressed his lips to mine again. "So at this rate you might be signing up for marathons."

"Not funny!" I leaned back and chucked a pillow at him. "Running is stupid."

He chuckled and put his arm along the back of the couch. "Well, it looks like that walk on the Greenbelt is going to have to wait."

I leaned into his chest and felt his warmth seep through my sweater. "Sorry, it sounded great."

He shrugged. "We can go later, once you are better."

I felt his chest expand as he yawned. He had started working late after he left my apartment a few times this week, and I was positive he wasn't getting the doctor-recommended number of hours of sleep. That, plus the contractors and collectors were constantly calling. I was worried for him.

His fingers were firm yet gentle as they rubbed my scalp and played with my hair. *Later.* He was planning on a later with me. I wondered how much later? I loved every minute we spent together, but a part of me was waiting for the other shoe to drop.

There would be something.

Another girl.

Work taking all his focus.

He would change his mind about me.

It could be a million things, but each one led to heartbreak.

I rubbed the smooth button of his blue button-up shirt. He had another Kismet event tonight in a few hours, but he came to sit with me until it started.

Somehow without me noticing, and without my permission, Grant had become the person I talked to before I fell asleep and the first one I texted in the morning.

How had this man already made such an imprint on my heart when we had been together for only six days? He had shown me how it felt to be appreciated for who I was. The cuddles and make-outs were not bad either.

Grant shifted under me, causing me to look at his face. "Hey, are you okay? Does your ankle hurt?"

I shook my head. "Sorry, I was just thinking about how it's crazy I haven't known you that long."

He kissed my forehead, "It's been a pretty great week, though." He smiled, showing off his dimple.

"True."

He winked. "Let me grab some fresh ice." He carefully unwound me from his chest, leaning me back onto the couch.

He walked to the kitchen, and I pictured how it would feel for him to be walking away for good. My heart buckled at the thought. My breath hitched, and I knew if it ended, it would take a long while to recover.

"Want me to start a movie? I'm sure you have more Cary Grants." He raised his brows as he dumped the ice in the sink and grabbed some fresh ice from the freezer.

Maybe the Grant from the movies I was looking for did exist.

He came in a little different packaging than I expected, with a love of rock music and a weird addiction to pickle chips and Red Bull. But he was just as kind and loving as I'd imagined.

He was standing in my kitchen right now, even though he was so busy. He was here now, asking to watch my favorite movie. He was here now to take care of me. Was it too good to be true?

"*Roman Holiday* is great. Not Cary Grant, though."

He shrugged. "Your call." He gingerly placed the ice on my ankle, adjusting the pillow underneath it. "When did you last take ibuprofen?"

I picked up my phone, glancing at the time. "Two hours ago."

He nodded and sat beside me, handing me the remote.

I didn't get to know the ending from the start, but the start was turning out to be something amazing. I turned on *Roman Holiday*. "Next we can do the *Transformers* one?"

He put his arm behind me. "Deal. That one might have to wait until after work, though."

I nodded and leaned my head onto his chest. "Did you know *Roman Holiday* was Audrey Hepburn's first major role? It was also the first rom-com to win an Academy Award for Best Story."

Grant chuckled behind me, then his lips pressed against my hair and he rested his jaw on top of my head. He was asleep within fifteen minutes.

OVER THE NEXT WEEK, THERE WERE MORE MOVIES, talks of our families, hopes we had for the future, and lots of kissing.

Friday after I closed up The Bees Knees, I walked to my car. Grant was supposed to have the movie for the event next Wednesday. Mr. Cole was putting more pressure on him. I wasn't sure it was in his job description, but he just said that what Mr. Cole wanted, he got.

I climbed into my yellow Bug and pulled out of the parking garage. I headed out to Mom's. She needed some help with some spring cleanup. This week the garbage trucks would take bigger items for free, and she asked me to come help.

I knocked on the door before I pushed it open. "Hey Mom, it's me."

Spike hissed and ran toward the laundry room. I guess he never forgave me for the spray paint or subsequent enforced washing. I walked into the kitchen of my childhood and memories rushed at me: making a swing out of the cabinet handles, a small wooden table that I scratched my name into one day when I was mad, and the burn mark on the countertop from the time I didn't think I needed a hot pad.

"In the living room," Mom called. I walked past the wall plastered with school pictures and art projects through the years. Stepping through this hall felt like falling back in time. Back to when the house was full of loud voices. The worn brown carpet showed years of coming and going.

But now, it was just Mom's footsteps in this big house.

"Hey, Mom." I found her in the living room going through boxes of food magazines, with *Fiddler on the Roof* playing on the TV in the background. She was picking up each magazine, looking through, and ripping out pages of recipes I knew she would never make. "What can I help with?"

She patted the faded blue couch cushion beside her. "Want to help me rip out recipes?"

"I thought you said you needed me to help?"

She patted the couch harder; I chuckled and sat. She handed me a stack of twenty years of magazines. I flipped open the first one stuffed with Easter recipes. "Mom, there is a recipe on almost every page."

"After you rip them out, put them in the piles." She pointed at the table. "Main course," she moved her hand down the line, "sides, and then desserts."

I wanted to argue it wasn't worth her time with the internet, but I also didn't want to fight tonight. So I sat and ripped page after page, listening to Reb Tevye.

"So, how are things going with Grant?"

"You could have called and asked." I bumped into her with my shoulder.

"I'm your mother. I shouldn't have to call." Her eyes scrunched. "Besides, I have fifteen years of magazines to go through, and you scammed me."

Yep. I think she would be able to use that one for years still and I would do whatever she asked. If this wasn't the definition of cruel and unusual punishment, I did not know what was.

"I think things are going well with Grant." I turned the page. "He has been amazing, actually." I tried to contain the smile begging to be released. "I'm still a little worried it can't last, though."

Mom smiled. "That's because you are like me." She raised her brows. "Once you decide something, it takes a whole lot to change your mind."

I nodded. That did fit us both to a T. I sighed and ripped out an apple stuffing recipe. "He is super sweet." I nodded to the TV. "Even if he hated *Fiddler* when he was younger."

Mom chuckled. "Even you hated *Fiddler*. It's one that gets better with age." She picked up another magazine. "So, have you kissed?"

"Mom!" I scoffed. "We don't need to go over all the details."

She clapped and squealed. "You *have* kissed."

I rolled my eyes. "Okay, you win. Yes. I like him." I sighed and thought of how he made my heart race. "I like him a lot."

Mom gestured for me to keep talking.

"I feel like I can talk to him forever, and time stands still and goes quickly at the same time. It seems crazy. I have only been spending time with him for two weeks. He doesn't belittle me or seem annoyed by my fashion sense. He watches my movies and helped me at The Bees Knees the other day when I needed some things moved around. But it's more than that. I like that he lets me in, too. He isn't wrapped up in others' opinions, talks to me for an hour about some new workout equipment, and tells me about work. It feels real."

"Sounds like someone is in love." Mom raised her brows.

My hands froze mid rip.

Was I in love? I thought about him and how he made me smile. When he wasn't with me, I felt like something was missing. Even now at the thought of him, my heart would skip a beat. If I didn't love him yet, I was standing on the edge, getting ready to jump.

Hm.

"I'm happy for you, hon."

"Mom, things are still super early." I raised my hand to stop the train before it left the station.

"Real love isn't about how long you've known someone—it's about how they make you feel about yourself. Do they make you a better, more confident version of yourself when you're with them? Do they help you believe in yourself and what you can accomplish, and do you get to do those things for them? Real love is the stuff the movies wish they could capture."

Grant made me feel special and more confident.

I finished ripping the page. "Do you want these chocolate cupcakes to go in dessert or main course?" I showed the picture of chocolate cupcake swirled masterpieces.

She rolled her eyes. "Honestly, Emma. Main course for sure," and then we both giggled.

"So, what about the guy that you met at Kismet? The one that recognized you. Have you seen him again?"

Mom lifted her right shoulder. "Hm, I don't think I can remember."

The sparkle in her eyes said something very different.

Chapter Thirteen

I stood behind the counter of The Bees Knees, spinning the bottle cap of my Dr. Pepper. I watched it spin in circles before it fell flat on the counter.

Everything always falls. I was foolish to believe otherwise.

I checked my phone for the hundredth time today. No new calls or texts from Grant. It had been four days since I realized I was falling in love with him, and the same four days since he pulled away. I was so glad I hadn't said anything about my realization to him.

I spun the bottle cap again and watched it fall. He'd called Sunday night and said he had some unexpected repairs at work, and he needed to cancel our plans. I wasn't worried. I thought he meant plans for the next day. I figured he would call that night. He didn't, and he hadn't called since.

My chest squeezed tighter. I should have stuck to setting up other people. Why had I let everyone change my mind that this was better?

I walked over to the record player and picked up the needle, silencing Elvis. I set the tonearm on the player handle. If I listened to Elvis now, every time I listened in the future, I would think of

Grant. I would rebuild the barrier around my heart, but I wouldn't let him ruin the King for me, too. I was exhausted, and it was only 8 a.m. on Wednesday.

I plopped into the yellow velvet swivel chair, my body sinking deeper than the chair should allow. The exhaustion wasn't just physical; it was in my bones, deep in my soul, and refused to leave. My limbs felt heavy, my heart heavier. I couldn't replay every interaction over more than I had. Was his hug more distant than before? Was his goodbye faster?

I reread our recent text thread as I turned the chair. I looked for a hidden sign or pivotal shift—a moment in time I could pinpoint at why or when things changed. But it was the same since Sunday, a handful of one-word texts, few and very far between.

I leaned back in the seat and rested my head. I wished I'd let go gracefully. I texted way more than socially acceptable and even left a few ridiculous voicemails about how I was worried, wondering if he was okay.

Nothing. I cringed as I thought of him listening to any one of my three voicemails. Desperate and clingy.

It had only been three weeks since our first date. How had my heart shifted toward him so hard in three weeks?

I typed out another text.

Emma: Grant, things feel off. Are you okay? Are we okay?

I rubbed my forehead and realized I wrote that text a few days ago and got no reply. I sighed and deleted the text.

Was it too early to delete the selfies of us on my phone and hope the attached memories would fade just as easily?

I leaned forward, resting my elbows on my knees and wiped my hands down my face. Trying to erase the lines of pain and tears.

Grant had moved on.

I sank deeper into my chair, wishing it could swallow me whole and let me just disappear into nothingness.

The ding of the front door had me sitting up, looking in

earnest for a man I already told my heart I didn't care about. Jane stood at the door, searching for me.

"Over here." I sighed. She followed the broken sound to find me planted in a chair, and I would only get up when necessary.

"Still nothing?" Her eyebrows creased as she sat in the chair beside me.

"Nope." I set my phone on the coffee table in front of me so I would stop checking it. "Unless you count a few very short 'sorry can't, work' texts, it's gone completely silent."

Jane pinched her lips and tipped her head in thought. "He never did anything or said anything to make you think his feelings had changed?"

I gestured toward my phone. "You are welcome to read the texts, but honestly, I can't think of anything. The last time we were together was Saturday night. It seemed like all the others."

"What did you guys do?" Jane's eyes searched through our last few days of texts.

I closed my eyes, preparing to reopen the wound as we hashed out the exchange again. "We walked around shops at The Village." I pinched the bridge of my nose. "We walked under the white twinkle lights, sat by the different fireplaces, and watched the water fountain show."

"Did he still kiss you and hold your hand?"

"Yep. Literally everything was the same." I threw my hands in the air. "I can't figure it out Jane, I've tried."

She handed me my phone and leaned back. "Hm. Does he know how you feel about him?"

"I mean, I thought so." I stood, no longer able to sit still. "We hadn't defined ourselves as boyfriend girlfriend or anything, but I thought we were close to it." I shifted back and forth.

"I mean...maybe it's all in my head?" I rubbed my forehead, trying to ease the oncoming headache. "Maybe work is taking a lot? It just feels like it is very different."

Jane stood and walked toward me before pulling me into a

hug. She stepped back and put her hands on my shoulders. "So, what are you going to do about it?"

"What do you mean?" I stepped back. "I called and I texted. It feels like the ball is in his court."

"Emma," Jane pressed her steepled fingers to her mouth. "What if he got scared that his feelings aren't reciprocated?"

I raised my brows and shook my head. "I doubt it. Based on the make-out we had Saturday, he knew."

Jane shook her head. "Not necessarily. Actions and words can mean different things for different people."

"I don't know..." My throat tightened. "It feels more like he decided to ghost me, versus telling me 'we're going in different directions.'" I used air quotes.

"This is the most you have liked someone in years." She reached to the box of tissues on the coffee table, handing me a tissue to wipe a tear I couldn't even feel. "But Em, this guy feels different. You feel different." She stepped back to look me in the eyes. "Are you sure you are willing to walk away without ever knowing?"

I sighed and shook my head. "What would I do? Even if I wanted to see him, he always came to my house. Other than stalking the gym he goes to, I wouldn't even know how to find him." I rubbed my temples. "Which has me wondering if he planned on this all along."

Jane raised her left brow. "You know where he works. If he is busy, go help him."

I shook my head. "What if I go and he gets in more trouble with Cole?"

She put her hand on her hip. "Surely Cole isn't always there."

I sat back down in my seat, feeling the weight of my true fear. "What if I go and he doesn't want to see me?" I whispered and looked to the ground. "What if he isn't busy at work, but no longer wants me?"

Jane snapped her fingers. "Girl, if that's the case, then you deserve WAY more than that, but he needs to put on his big boy pants and tell you."

I rubbed a hand over my lips. "I don't know that I want him to." I melted.

Jane kneeled in front of me. "You need to fight for the people you love and the way you deserve to be treated." She raised my chin. "He is either drowning in work and will be relieved to see you, or he is a jerk and I hope Cole is there and runs him through the wringer."

I closed my eyes, needing space between myself and the dangerous idea of going to The Brick House to see for myself how things were between us.

"I don't know. Maybe it's best to just let it fade and forget. Go back to setting people up. It was far less complicated and painful."

Jane quirked an eyebrow. "Yeah? You wish you never felt what it was like to kiss Grant?"

Did I wish I never had that memory? I replayed each kiss and touch. Nope. Even if I was old and single, I would want to remember each brush of his fingers, every kiss.

"Do you wish you never knew how it felt to be held by him? Or the way he validated you and made you feel seen?"

I never wanted to forget that.

I pinched my lips and shook my head. "No."

Even if it was over, I never wanted to forget the way he made me feel. How he made me believe it was possible to be myself and be loved at the same time.

"Emma, do you think he is worth fighting for or not?" Jane grabbed my shoulders. "Love is like the best piece of cake in the world, and cake like that does not have a shelf life. If you don't take it, someone else will."

I bit my bottom lip. I did love cake. I wanted things to work between Grant and me, but I also wanted to make sure he was okay, even if we weren't.

"Maybe?"

Jane pulled me into a tight hug. "This is perfect!"

"Whoa." I held my hands up, "I don't know, I'm still thinking."

Jane raised her brows. "Oh, this is happening, and we will make you look so irresistible that he will instantly remember why he misses you or regret that he doesn't deserve you."

I took a deep breath and steeled my shoulders. I nodded my head in affirmation. Yes. I would go see him. I would see if he was okay, and then face whether we were done or not.

JANE BROUGHT ME MY FAVORITE HIGH WAISTED JEANS and red top, the ones that showed off my curves in the best way. I refreshed my makeup and hair and rushed out of work.

It was a Wednesday, but most of the Kismet activities didn't start until after 7 p.m., and it was just past five. I pulled into the parking lot of The Brick House. I took a deep breath, filling my lungs and slowly letting it out.

It would be worth the pain and discomfort to know. To know if Grant was doing okay and to know where we stood.

I stiffened my shoulders and added a layer of Grant's favorite lip gloss. No reason I shouldn't put my best foot forward, so to speak. I stepped out of the car and headed to the concrete steps.

Was Jane right?

Was this fighting for us to work?

Or was this just asking for more pain?

Did he already give me my answer?

At least this was me not running. This was me trying. If nothing else, Mom and Jane would be proud.

My hands shook and my heart was racing. I took another breath and pulled open the doors.

The warm wood and metal accents felt familiar but impersonal at the same time. When Grant's hand was in mine, it felt safe, but standing in the foyer with groups of people hustling about, it felt cold.

I expected the place to be mainly empty. I looked back to the glass double doors. Should I leave?

I heard him—a voice that had felt safe and a lot like home. Grant was facing the other direction in a blue button-up and suit pants and was gesturing to someone in front of him, and based on his shoulders, he was not happy.

This didn't look like the best time after all. Last chance to run.

I could go back to my car and pretend like I didn't care.

I did not do my hair for nothing.

Besides, if I did that, then I would never know. I'd always wonder what had caused the sudden shift between us. I steeled my shoulders. I deserved an answer.

I stepped closer. The man Grant was talking to locked eyes with me, eyes that were cold and angry. Darian Cole.

I felt an icy chill run down my spine.

"For some reason, I don't believe you." Mr. Cole gestured toward me.

I stepped closer as Grant turned around. His eyes found mine and went from confused to frustrated.

"Maybe if you weren't spending your time with a certain gold digger, you could actually have a successful business. You would have caught it sooner, and you would have prioritized keeping your client, your only client, happy." He slapped his hands together causing a sharp sound. Grant flinched. "Your father was right. You'll never amount to anything because you aren't willing to do what it takes. I don't know why I let you convince me to give you a chance."

"Hey!" I was furious with Grant, but I wasn't going to let this man sit here and talk to him like that. "Maybe if you weren't actually a jerk, you wouldn't have to trick a whole town of single ladies into trying to give you a chance."

Mr. Cole stepped to the side, so he had a clear path to me. His fists were clenched, and a vein had started to pulse on his forehead. "You want to say that again?"

I now understood the saying "if looks could kill." I took a half step back before I reminded myself I wouldn't let this bully push me around.

Grant stepped over, blocking Cole's path. "Emma, you need to leave." He didn't even care enough to look at me, just yelled over his shoulder.

"I just wanted to see you, I thought you might need help. You said you would call and—"

"Emma, go. Now," Grant quipped over his shoulder. "You said you wouldn't show up at Kismet events."

I raised my chin higher. "I did, and you said that you wanted to give us a try, and a bunch of work-life balance crap. So, I guess we both lied."

Jane was wrong. He hadn't wanted to see me. He had cut contact on purpose.

Darian Cole growled. "Someone ought to teach that woman some manners."

Grant stiffened and stepped closer to Cole. "Emma, leave. Now." His voice was sharp—louder than necessary. Angrier than I'd ever heard.

Any hope I'd held on to shattered like glass. I'd tricked myself into believing that Grant would want to see me or at least have an explanation. Instead I was met with his cold anger, and I knew if we had anything previously, it was long gone.

I forced my chin higher, even as my throat tightened. "I know the way out." My voice didn't crack, not yet. "Don't worry. You'll never see me again."

I turned, pushing through the double doors before the first tear could fall.

The evening air was cold against my skin, but not as cold as Grant's dismissal.

My fingers fumbled for my keys; I couldn't see through the blur of tears. My breath hitched, shallow and frantic. I needed to leave. Now. Before the sob in my throat broke free. I was totally throwing away this outfit. I ran to my car and drove out of the parking lot.

Jane and Mom had been wrong.

I should have never come.

I should have never tried.

I should have never loved.

Chapter Fourteen

I PUT MY CAR INTO PARK ON THE LONG GRAVEL driveway and reached for another package of tissues. I ripped it open, my hands shaking. My breath came in sharp, hiccupping gasps that deprived my lungs of air. My chest ached, raw and hollow, as if my heart had shattered into something too sharp to fit back together.

I tried.

And it still didn't work. I still wasn't wanted.

No one stayed, no one wanted me.

My throat burned with unshed sobs.

The sharp rap on the window jolted me, snapping me out of the spiral. I turned, my vision blurred, to see Mom standing there, her brow furrowed in worry.

She tried the door, but it was still locked. I hit the unlock button and mom pulled the door open. She squatted down beside me so we were eye level.

"What's wrong?"

I blew my nose into my tissue. "Oh nothing..." I gasped, trying to catch my breath. "It's just you and Jane were both wrong." My head flopped onto the steering wheel as I choked back a sob. "It didn't work out and now I am miserable. I was fine before. I was content." I blew my nose into another tissue.

Mom's hand moved in slow, soothing circles on my back, smoothing out the cracks in me one stroke at a time. "It's cold," she said gently and nodded toward her house. "Let's go inside." She reached over and took my hand in hers, and pulled me from the car.

I followed her inside, my body shuddering with sharp stabs of pain in my chest.

Sitting at the worn kitchen table, I closed my eyes and tried to calm down. Love wasn't worth the pain.

"Okay, let's talk about it." Mom scooted her chair closer and pulled my face toward her, her arms extended, and she waited for me.

"Oh, Mom." I buried my face into her as I wrapped my arms around her in a hug, smearing the contents leaking from my face onto her shirt.

"What happened?" Mom pulled me in tighter.

She wouldn't let me fall, she wouldn't leave, because she truly loved me. "I ruined everything." I reached for another tissue.

Mom wiped the tears off my cheeks. "Oh, I doubt that. But just in case," she stood from the table and headed over to the cabinet. "I have never faced a problem that couldn't be softened with some chocolate." She smiled as she reached into the cupboard and pulled out a battered plastic container—the same one from my childhood, still decorated with fading broccoli stickers.

I let out a watery laugh. "You still keep it in there?"

Mom shrugged. "It helps me not eat it as fast, plus I like the memories it brings with it." She grabbed a bowl and put some mini candy bars in it and then grabbed an extra box of tissues. "I used to change up the hiding place to see how long it would take for you little heathens to find my chocolate stash." She chuckled. "It was never long." She sat beside me, pushing the bowl of chocolate toward me. "Let's start at the beginning."

I folded my arms over my chest trying to hold everything together. "Everything hurts. I let myself hope. I let myself believe that love could work for me. I don't know why I agreed to date him." I picked up a Snickers as I gasped for breath. "I was so stupid."

"That's not stupid, hon." She pulled me into a side hug before she reached for a chocolate.

"No, it was." I nodded, resolute. "Love might work for other people, but it's not for us."

Mom leaned back. "What do you mean?"

"Dad left before I could hardly walk, and you haven't loved anyone else since. You know every relationship is a ticking time bomb, waiting to end."

"Emma." Mom smiled. "I have loved and been loved every day of my life." She raised her brows.

I scoffed and leaned away. "It doesn't count if it's us kids."

She scowled. "Why ever not? You have filled my life with so much love and hope. I never had a day I didn't feel love. Plus, I have had a few romantic relationships since your father as well." Mom exhaled, setting her chocolate down. "And your dad didn't leave us. I made him leave."

The words didn't compute at first. I blinked at her, my breath catching in my throat. "Wait...what?"

"Oh, Emma, if you focus too close on the piece in front of you, you will never get to see the whole picture." She picked up my hand in hers. "But I can promise you I have love, by you and others. I loved your dad, even if we ended up not working out."

"Wait, you made Dad leave?" My brain was spiraling.

Mom's shoulders drooped. "Your father was constant proof you can love something that is not good for you." She reached up and brushed a tear off my cheek. "I know a little about choosing to love yourself over the pretend affections of a man." Her head tipped lower to see my eyes. "But I also know what it feels like to be loved for who you are, not in spite of it."

I didn't know if it was from the tears or incoming headache but I was spinning. I didn't know Mom left Dad, or that she had dated through the years. In fact, sitting here at this table with the wonderful woman holding me, I wasn't sure if I knew my mother at all.

"Love is worth the risk." She straightened her shoulders. "Now, enough about your father and my love life." She patted my back. "What happened to you and Grant?"

This beautiful woman with wrinkles and worn hands had always been there when I needed her. "I love you, Mom."

She pulled me into another hug. "Love you too, Em, but you're not getting out of it that easy."

I chuckled. "I know. I just wasn't sure I told you enough." I leaned my head onto her shoulder and absorbed the weight of her head resting against mine.

"Probably not." I felt her chuckle.

I took a strong breath and started to spill every piece of my shattered heart. She sat there and listened. Not interrupting or judging, just listening.

Once I went over what happened earlier that evening, I felt sick to my stomach. "I was hoping I wouldn't get him in trouble. I was hoping I could help him. I just got this idea in my head that maybe he needed help and wanted to see me." I shook my head in defeat. "But I was so, so wrong."

Mom sat quietly putting her thoughts into place. "I'm sorry about your night, hon, but it also isn't all on you." She met my eyes, with raised brows. "You did deserve answers, and you did not intend to cause him trouble." She pinched her lips and rubbed my hand. "You never know. Tonight might not be as final as you feel." She wiped a tear from my cheek and pulled me into an embrace. I felt my gasping breaths matching her steady heartbeat, calming my storm.

"No, it is. I even told him I never wanted to see him again as I ran out."

Mom continued to rub my back in soft circles. "Maybe." She shrugged. "Time has taught me a lot of things, and one is that the word *never* is not as final as it seems. And if it doesn't work between you and Grant, it wasn't supposed to, but that doesn't mean you don't have more love coming your way." She leaned back and looked at me. "Now, want to watch a movie?"

I nodded. "Yeah." I stood and turned toward the living room. I walked in and sat on the corner cushion of the worn blue couch. Mom walked to the back of the room, grabbing my favorite green blanket from the stack and bringing it to me. "All right, which movie are we feeling tonight?"

I grabbed the soft blanket and tugged it tightly around me, hoping the warmth would fill the hole in my chest. The familiar scents wrap around me like a second embrace—lavender laundry soap, faint traces of sun-dried hay, and something indefinably Mom.

The blanket was healing, but mostly it was Mom that was healing, as she held me close, letting me know I was safe and loved no matter what. Her lips pressed against my forehead as I leaned against her, watching the opening credits to the movie.

Chapter Fifteen

THE NEXT TWO DAYS WERE FULL OF TISSUES AND chocolate—lots of chocolate—but I recovered.

I still loved Grant, but I could say I was glad I had tried.

I had learned about myself and that I could be myself and be loved.

I wanted Grant to be happy and also not in trouble for me showing up at his work. I felt I might never forgive myself if he ended up losing his business because of me.

I knew the Kismet Silvers movie showing was supposed to be starting soon, so I spent the day calling and driving all over to pick up the reels that had been set aside for me.

It wasn't a lot, but they were playable, and that seemed better than nothing.

I asked Mom if she would go to the Kismet Silvers event for me one last time, and she surprised me by saying she already had tickets for tonight.

I put my car into park in Mom's driveway and reached over to the passenger seat, grabbing the box beside me. It wasn't a bad collection. I added my DVD of *My Favorite Wife* for good measure. I couldn't find the reel, but I thought it might make Grant smile.

Okay, I admit it. I hoped it would bring him fond memories of us. I didn't want him to remember us from our last interaction.

It wouldn't fix everything, but hopefully it would fix things between him and Mr. Cole.

Mom opened the door with a smile. "Come on in. I'm almost ready." Mom was possibly looking younger than me at the moment. She seemed content. She seemed happy.

I stepped out of my car and walked into the house, setting the box on the table.

"Are you sure, Mom? You don't have to do this if you don't want to."

"Oh hush." She smiled. "Stop being so dramatic. I was already planning on going."

I pulled out my chair and sat. "Yeah, about that..."

"Oh no, don't you start." She raised her brows in challenge and placed her hands on her hips.

"Start what?" I asked in a high sweet voice. "I was only going to say that maybe you didn't hate going to them so much after all."

Mom rolled her eyes and went to grab her jacket. "I'm going to pretend you didn't say that." She pulled her jacket on and came up to me, bending to give me a hug. "I'm proud of you, Em. For trying to make things right with Grant, as well as giving love an honest try." She kissed me on top of my hair.

"I'm still not sure I'm ready to go through that again anytime soon." I crossed my arms over my chest.

"Life likes to be hard." Mom patted my cheeks and gave me a smile. "When it's not the way you want, keep pushing, and good things come. More often than not, it ends up better than you could have planned in the long run."

I thought about what I knew of Mom's past. She was the prime example of pushing through hard things and still hoping for good.

"Are you happy with how your life turned out?"

She rolled her eyes. "I'm not dead yet."

I raised my hands. "No, I know, I just meant..."

She chuckled. "Yes, I'm very happy with my life." She booped my nose. "With each of my beautiful babies and the joy they bring me, and I'm excited for the life I have yet to live." She winked.

There was a knock at the door and I stood to answer it. "Thanks again for doing this, Mom."

"You bet, hon." She followed behind me. "Now, you go enjoy your date with Leo's and pj's. But one day, you are going to pull yourself off that couch and put yourself back out there."

I nodded. "I love you."

"Love you too."

I reached the door and opened it. A man with gray hair and a square jawline was poised to knock again.

"Oh my!" He raised his hand to his heart. "You surprised me! Is Hannah here?" He tried to peek over my shoulder.

I raised an eyebrow and looked over my shoulder. "Mom?"

Where had I seen him before?

"Of course I'm here." A beautiful smile bloomed on Mom's face. "Would you mind grabbing this box for me, Robert?" She pointed to the box on the table.

I stepped to the side, allowing him access to Mom's house. I held the door as he walked up to Mom and gave her a hug. Then he lifted the box from the table.

"Thanks again for the ride, Robert."

"It's my pleasure." He grinned in my mom's direction, then walked out the front door I still held open.

A memory clicked into place and I snapped my fingers. "You're the guy from the Kismet thing!"

He grinned. "Guilty." He popped the trunk of his car and set the box inside.

Mom walked by me, smelling like lavender and sunshine. She raised her brows at me and bit back a smile.

I laughed and rolled my eyes. "Have fun!"

"We will," Mom called back.

Robert opened the door for her and then walked over to the driver's side. Mom waved to me as Robert backed the car out of the driveway.

I chuckled and shook my head.

Huh. I definitely needed to spend more time with my mother. She had some major tea to spill—apparently years of it.

I walked back to my car and smiled as I drove home. I unlocked my apartment and stepped inside. Everything looked the same but somehow felt different.

Maybe no relationship ever truly leaves. They all change us. Friends, boyfriends, teachers, and co-workers. Everyone that had touched my life had left a piece of themselves with me and changed my perspective.

I dressed in my silk Elvis pj's and called in the usual order of Leo's Pasta. If Peter brought extra cupcakes this time, I would happily eat them all.

Cupcakes.

How long would cupcakes remind me of kissing Grant for the first time?

Not helping.

I needed a distraction, so I turned on the TV. Looking at the recently watched movies, I clicked through, alternating between black-and-white and Marvel.

Ugh! It was like Grant was still everywhere I turned. I wiped a stray tear from my cheek. I had already decided I was done crying.

I would recover, and I would be grateful that Grant taught me I can be myself and still be deserving of love.

I tossed the remote on the couch. Maybe I should ask Jane if she wanted to go for a walk?

I felt my forehead for a temperature; surely things were not that drastic.

I lay down on the couch and closed my eyes. I would wake up

when Leo's got here, and that would help. I was always more dramatic when I was hungry.

I came out of my haze of a dream of cupcakes and geese and registered a knock at the door.

"Coming!" I hoped Peter hadn't been there long. I sat up and rubbed my eyes, hoping they seemed sleepy and not like I had been crying for days. I crossed the room to my purse. I grabbed it off the hook under the movie poster for *My Favorite Wife*, remembering my old habit of wishing on the Grant picture for my own Grant.

Reaching the front door, I pulled it open. "Sorry, I think I fell aslee—" My eyes locked onto a pair of familiar dark brown eyes. Grant stood there holding my food bags from Leo's with a sad look on his face. I gasped and threw the door closed.

"Emma?" Grant sounded nervous.

I leaned against the closed door.

What was he doing here?

"Please, Emma, let me in." Grant's voice carried through the door, broken and quiet.

I sighed as I held my body against the door. Was I ready to face him again? I turned and grabbed the handle, wondering if I should turn it or hold it closed.

"Emma, please. Just let me explain."

I steeled my shoulders. Of course I wanted to see him. I slowly opened the door and peeked out.

There he stood, looking as ever like a Greek god in his slacks and button-up shirt, except his shoulders drooped and there were bags under his eyes.

"Hey, Emma." He gave a sad smile. "Can I come in?" He held up the food. "Peter was here when I came, so I paid him and asked if I could bring it in." He shrugged his shoulders. "I hope that's okay."

I bit my lip and paused. I looked at the bags of food and his broken posture. I sighed and opened the door farther. "I don't understand..."

Grant stepped in slowly, his eyes on mine.

I took a few steps away, watching him cautiously, my arms folded tight around myself to keep from reaching out to him. "I'm sorry if I got you in trouble, Grant. I did plan on seeing if I could help you." I looked to the floor.

Grant walked over to the coffee table and put the food down. He turned to face me. "No, Emma." He sighed and looked up to the ceiling. "You have nothing to apologize for. It was all my fault." He shook his head. "I got caught up in work again. I had one crisis after another. Water lines, failed credit loans, and then Cole." He pinched the bridge of his nose. "Each morning I told myself I would call you, and then each night as I left work at 3 a.m. I felt like it was too late." His voice broke. "Then it started to feel too long, that a quick call or text couldn't validate any of it."

I took in his appearance. "Work!" I looked at the clock. It was in the middle of the Kismet event. "Grant! You need to go." I pushed him toward the door. "Mr. Cole will be furious. You'll lose everything. We definitely need to have this conversation, and this time you will call me back." I raised my eyebrows, to let him know I was serious. "But we can do it later."

Grant stood straight and shook his head. "No."

I sighed. "Grant, what about Mr. Cole?"

"I don't care about him."

I sighed again more softly. "Maybe you think you don't, but I know you do."

He touched my shoulders. "If I have to become like my father or Mr. Cole for my business to succeed, it's not worth saving." His jaw clenched, and he shook his head. "I need to succeed while being kind, succeed while having balance for other people in my life, succeed by being my own man."

"Are you sure?" I whispered.

"I need to be here, now. Please let me finish. Then I will go if you want." He rubbed a tear off my cheek. "I treated you so badly that night." He crumpled, leaning against the wall as he slid to the floor. I sat cross-legged in front of him. "I was scared. I was scared of who I was becoming. I was so angry at Cole." His jaw clenched, and he put a fist to his forehead. "And when he turned his venom on you—" He looked at me, really looked at me. "I thought he was going to hurt you, and I saw red. I wanted to hit him. I wanted to hurt him." His voice broke and his jaw tightened.

I saw Grant as a little boy with an angry father, a boy that wanted his father's love and sought his approval so much that it ruled his life even now. My heart ached for him and the hurt he still carried. I reached over and rubbed the back of his hand.

He turned his palm and held my hand in his, staring at our touch.. "Then I watched you run away, saying you never wanted to see me again." Tears ran down his face. "That moment was proof. I was just like my dad." He shook his head. "A man I hated and vowed never to be." He met my gaze, sad and broken. "I yelled at you and hurt you, just like he was always hurting my mom." He wiped his tears. "At that moment, I hated everything about me. I still hate everything about me." He crumpled further.

"Grant..."

I was starting to make peace with the decision that Grant wasn't in my life anymore; this was not helping.

He gave me a sad smile. "I chose that day to change. I went to The Bees Knees twice, but couldn't go in. My mom told me to order you cupcakes, but on the way to your place, I decided you were better off without me and threw them away. I felt like I didn't deserve another chance."

Aww, he came to see me and talked to his mom about me. I reached over and took his other hand, interlacing our fingers.

"When your mom brought me that box, I knew." He pressed the back of my hand against his lips and leaned into the touch. "I knew I would never forgive myself if I didn't at least try. Emma, can you forgive me? I don't deserve another chance with you, but I can't not try."

My heart was racing, and I felt like I was going to cry. This beautiful man wanted me and he loved me. I could see it in his eyes, in the way he was desperately trying to pull me closer. I stared at his lips.

I smiled at him, tears now running down my face as well. For a man of not many words, tonight he'd professed quite a bit.

I didn't want the ending that I had written for us, I wanted a different one.

He was here right now, possibly at the cost of everything he cared about. He leaned, resting his forehead against mine with his eyes closed. "Mom suggested I go to therapy. I'm sure she's right."

The corner of my lips turned up in a smile. "Jane suggested therapy for me too." I shrugged and ducked my head to make eye contact with him. "Grant, make sure." I sighed. This was not how I planned on having this conversation, but I needed him to know. I leaned back so I could gather my thoughts. "I think I'm falling in love with you, so please..." My breath caught in my throat. "Please, don't say things unless you are sure."

His fingertips were under my chin, lifting my gaze to his. "Emma." He scooted closer to me and ran his thumb down my face. "Emma, I'm in love with you." His eyes locked on to mine. "I felt like I was drowning before I met you. Drowning in anger, emptiness, and grief." His eyes brightened and he shook his head. "Then you came. This beautiful, strong, classy woman that turned my entire world upside down." One side of his mouth pulled up in a grin, flashing that dimple that I had been desperately missing.

I bit my bottom lip as I stared up into his bright eyes.

"I love you." He put his hands on the back of my neck. "If you don't want to give me a second chance, I will walk away." His voice broke as his eyes desperately searched mine. "But if you give me a second chance, I can't wait to prove to you how I can be different. I can be better."

"No more rules that I can't help you at work?" My eyebrows raised. "This is a big part of your life and I want to be a part of it, when possible."

"Deal." He nodded. "I promise to never go a whole day without answering you. Communication isn't a strong skill for me, but I will try."

This man was flawed and broken, just like me but in different ways. Maybe together we could help fix some of the broken pieces we had hidden inside.

I held my hand out for him, and he placed his in mine. I stood and led him over to the couch. He touched my shoulder, and I turned to face him.

"Emma." He stepped closer, his chest pressed up against mine. "I want to spend every second with you," he whispered as he put his hand gently on the back of my neck, his thumb rubbing along my jaw. "I want to make you smile and tell you I love you over and over again."

"Do you know if Peter added any cupcakes?" I parted my lips and winked.

He glanced at my lips. "I'm going to need an actual answer, Emma." His smile was wicked. "I don't want to overstep, and I'm seconds from pulling you into my arms and never letting you go. I have missed the way you fit into my arms, the way you fit into my heart."

I went up on my tiptoes and brushed my lips over his neck. "Then, I guess maybe we won't need the cupcakes after all," I whispered.

He chuckled and leaned into my touch.

"I forgive you, Grant, and I think we should give us another try."

He leaned back so his eager brown eyes could stare into mine. He rubbed his thumb along my cheek and one of his hands trailed down my back until it was on my waist. "Are you sure..."

I nodded, unable to contain my smile.

"In that case." He quirked an eyebrow and pulled me tight against him and pressed his lips to mine.

Our first kiss was passionate and fun, but this was different. It felt almost sacred. Like I was slowly putting his whole world back together, just like he was doing to mine. I wrapped my arms around him, pulling him tighter.

"I have missed you," he whispered against my neck. "I love you, Emma."

"I love you, Grant." I felt like I was melting and flying all at the same time.

Maybe real love isn't about grand romantic gestures like in the movies, but about choosing each other every day, to apologize and try again, in the messy moments of everyday life.

Looked like my mother was quite wrong about one thing. Some very good things can come from staying home in my pj's and ordering takeout.

THE END

Epilogue

I checked my hair in the visor mirror of my yellow Bug, tying half of it back with a blue silk ribbon that matched my dress. I swiped on a quick layer of pink lip gloss, took a deep breath, and grabbed my purse.

As I crossed the parking lot of The Brick House, butterflies swarmed my stomach. The same teenager stood at the entrance, that I had snuck past before, popping her bubblegum and scanning tickets. Only this time, it wasn't an event for the fifty-plus crowd.

Grant had come up with the idea to host a vintage movie night for the community and suggested The Bees Knees be the sponsor. Our first—of hopefully many—joint projects.

"Hey, Kelsey."

She waved me by without much acknowledgment. I chuckled, climbed the concrete steps, and walked inside the building.

The air smelled like popcorn, salt, and butter. My eyes immediately found my Mr. Muscles behind the bar, handing out bottled sodas, licorice ropes, and popcorn to eager kids.

I resisted the urge to skip as I hurried past the mingling crowd, making my way to Grant. Relief settled in my chest—people had actually showed up. For a while, I was worried it would be just Grant and me. Though, honestly, that didn't sound like a bad night either.

When I was almost at his side, I saw it—the exact moment he spotted me. His brown eyes lit up, his dimple appeared, and just like that, the butterflies in my stomach settled.

He stepped away from the counter, leaving the others to fill orders, and met me halfway.

"You're gorgeous," he murmured, pulling me into his arms and wrapping me in the scent of leather and earth.

My head tipped back, my cheeks aching from smiling. "Look at this." I gestured around the lobby. "I wasn't sure other people would even come."

His thumb brushed my cheek. "Of course they would. It was my idea."

I rolled my eyes. "Uh, my store is the sponsor, so I think it's a we event."

"You'll never hear me argue against anything we." He grinned, glancing at the black-and-white movie posters hanging throughout the lobby. "Just think—if it weren't for old movie reels, I never would've found you." His hand slid to my hip, pulling me closer, his grin turning delicious.

And then he kissed me, right there in the middle of the lobby.

The world melted away.

This man was everything. He made me believe in myself. He made me feel beautiful. Seen. Loved—in a way no one ever had.

When the kiss ended, he laced his fingers through mine.

"All right, we can't be late to our Cary Grant movie date." He raised a brow and nodded toward the ballroom. "Have you ever seen *My Favorite Wife?*"

"Oh, that sounds familiar, but I'm not sure."

I kissed him on my favorite dimple, and then caught a glimpse of someone across the lobby. Was that Peter from Leo's with, I guessed, his wife? I couldn't believe he was here. He gave me an excited wave.

Next to him, other familiar people. My mouth dropped open. What?

Ivy. Caleb. Mom—and Grant's mom, chatting like they were best friends. Mom's Robert also stood slightly behind my mother near the group.

"No way." I grabbed Grant's hand. I rushed over to them, dragging Grant. "You guys!" My heart swelled. "I can't believe you're here!"

Grant's mom blinked rapidly, dabbing at her eyes with a tissue. My forehead creased. Ivy grabbed my hand, pulling my attention to her as she pulled me into a hug.

Grant gave quick side hugs to Ivy and Caleb. "Thanks for coming."

"How long are you stay—"

Before I could finish, Jane ambushed me in a squealing hug.

"Em! This is amazing!"

"I know, right?" My cheeks hurt from smiling.

Grant cleared his throat, pulling everyone's attention. "All right, we better head inside. The movie's about to start."

Caleb clapped Grant on the back, and I caught the flicker of something on Grant's face—nerves?

We made our way inside, where the ballroom had been transformed into a classic movie theater—red ropes, red carpet, and rows of seats. A huge screen on the stage.

The lights dimmed, and orchestra music swelled through the speakers. The screen flickered to life, shifting through cards of actors and actresses.

Cary Grant was good-looking, don't get me wrong. But if I had to pick? My Grant won, all day, every day.

Grant lifted our joined hands and pressed a soft kiss to the back of mine. His breath was a little unsteady, his posture stiff. Was he worried about the event? Or was it something else?

Halfway through the movie, he leaned in close. "You know, I think you'd be my favorite wife."

I smacked his arm. "I'd better be your favorite—and only—wife." I raised an eyebrow in challenge.

He chuckled and then suddenly a light flicked on in the ballroom.

Confused, I turned toward the light switches. The movie was still playing, but...no one was watching it.

They were watching me. A hush had fallen over the room. My pulse kicked up. What...was happening?

I turned to Grant—only to find his seat empty.

My stomach tightened and I looked down.

There he was—kneeling in front of me, a small velvet box in his hand.

My breath caught.

"Emma Ann Woods," Grant cleared his throat and took a steadying breath. He opened his palm, waiting for me to take his hand.

Oh. My. Gosh. He was proposing?

My vision blurred as tears filled my eyes. The whole room, the whole world, faded to just him. Just this moment.

"You love your black-and-white movies," he said, a grin playing on his lips.

"True." I chuckled.

"I've decided that's because you are so full of color. So full of life. That's what you are to me—all the color. All the brightness."

I used my shoulder to wipe an errant tear on my cheek.

"Emma Ann Woods." His brown eyes found mine, and I got lost in the depth of them. "Would you do me the honor of becoming my favorite"—his lips quirked up—"and only wife?"

I pressed a hand to my heart, happy tears finally breaking free. "Yes! Yes! Yes!"

I stood up, pulling Grant with me, and threw my arms around him as the room erupted in cheers.

And just like that, I was home. Not a place. Not a building. Just him. Always him.

Acknowledgments

The amount of people it takes to help me put a book together will never cease to amaze me. I'm always surprised how much stronger my story becomes through the rounds of the editing process. That is largely because of a power team of women that cheer me on and call me out on my bad plot holes.

Melody Williams & Tanya Strong—my constant cheerleaders from the start of this crazy process. Thanks for the daily support and misguided belief in me. Thanks, ladies!

Casi Holman & Mandy Adamson—you're the ones that keep me writing. Your check-ins and writing meet-ups are my constant fuel. You push me to improve and stretch and I'm so lucky to have you both!

Ali Fields—Emma is so much stronger in this story now because of you. Thanks for pushing me and not letting me take the easy way out!

Lorren Lemmons—you are an angel, and the amount of grammar errors you find AFTER I do my best is purely embarrassing. Thanks!

Rachel Law—thanks for the crazy idea to have me on your sweet romance panel. This deadline has shown me I can achieve far more, at a faster rate than I ever imagined.

To my Joseph—the amount of romance books you read for me is astounding, especially for someone who hates reading. Thanks for the late plot chats, and conversations on our walks. I'm a better writer and a better person because you are in my life. All my love.

To my babies—sorry about the freezer meals and lack of

emotional awareness at times when I was tired. Ellie, thanks for the many talks of covers and sticker designs. Boys, thanks for not burning down the house while I was writing. I hope you all dream big always. Love you to pieces.

About the Author

Kiri Patterson grew up in small-town Idaho and communicates through movie quotes and song lyrics.

She taught herself to read before kindergarten and has loved reading ever since. Especially books with sweet love stories, strong characters, and lots of witty banter—ingredients she hopes to have in all her stories.

She tries to survive on chai, Dr. Pepper, and dark chocolate...but throws in the occasional vegetable for good measure. Other guilty pleasures include marathons of the Great British Baking Show, BBC period dramas, Harry Potter anything, and French fries.

Kiri currently resides in Star, Idaho, with her hot husband, four rapidly growing children, a strong belief in happily ever afters, and her pink laptop—a nod to her belief that everything is just a little better in pink.

Also by Kiri Patterson — *No Plans to Fall*